DR. MORELLE AT MIDNIGHT

Ian Laking is pathologically jealous of his beautiful wife, and obsessed with murder. His only hope lies in treatment by Dr. Morelle, the psychiatrist and criminologist. However Laking, suspecting his business associate Dyke Fenton of being his wife's lover, is plotting revenge . . . Dr. Morelle and his secretary, Miss Frayle, become caught up in the drama of jealousy and revenge. When the plan fatally recoils upon Laking himself, will Dr. Morelle be able to unmask the murderer?

ERNEST DUDLEY

DR. MORELLE
AT MIDNIGHT

Complete and Unabridged

LINFORD
Leicester

First published in Great Britain

First Linford Edition
published 2008

Copyright © 1959 by Ernest Dudley
All rights reserved

British Library CIP Data

Dudley, Ernest
    Dr. Morelle at midnight.—Large print ed.—
Linford mystery library
    1. Morelle, Doctor (Fictitious character)—
Fiction 2. Detective and mystery stories
    3. Large type books
    I. Title
    823.9'14 [F]

    ISBN 978–1–84782–067–9

Published by
F. A. Thorpe (Publishing)
Anstey, Leicestershire

Set by Words & Graphics Ltd.
Anstey, Leicestershire
Printed and bound in Great Britain by
T. J. International Ltd., Padstow, Cornwall

This book is printed on acid-free paper

1

The atmosphere of the operating-theatre was decidedly warm. A gleam of white walls, the glitter of bottles and winking instruments, even the autoclaves and washbasin taps seemed to pick up the brilliance of the green-white light.

A team of people stood round the operating-table under the intense heat of the 500-watt lamp. The table was draped with a green cloth. The patient was entirely covered in green towels. Except for the head. They called it the working area because the chief was operating on the brain. Green-robed, wearing white rubber boots, green cap, white gauze breathing-mask like every-one else in the theatre, he went skilfully to work.

On either side of the operating-table near the patient's head were instrument trolleys. These too were draped in green. Over the patient's head, on a high table,

scalpels and scissors winked in the brilliant lights.

The pretty brunette student staring down from the crowded, glass-enclosed students' gallery into the operating-theatre wondered inconsequently who the patient was. He could be a murderer, for all we know, she thought.

The surgeon's hand flickered. Instantly the senior dresser passed him the correct instrument. No word spoken. The silent language of hand signals.

The operation was at a critical stage. Lifting his eyes, one of the green-garbed figures glanced up and gazed round the theatre, he alone appeared detached, an observer. The pretty brunette whose attention had been oddly attracted by the tall figure before, perhaps because every-one else was vitally concerned with the operation, wondered who he was. She knew the short, dumpy man next to him. He was Sir Trevor Kirkland, famous neurologist; it looked as if the other was there by Sir Trevor's invitation to see the Swiss surgeon's new method of trepanning. The registrar, the house-surgeon,

the theatre sister, the anaesthetist, staff nurse, ward nurse, a team to back up the chief, a team with the most important job in the world, these she knew by sight.

A nurse passed that tall, detached figure carrying swabs. Green swabs, each with a fine metal line running through it, so that if by any ill chance one got left behind inside the patient, X-rays would soon pick it up. She began counting them, reported them all correct. She was concerned with nothing else. Just swabs.

Another nurse put used instruments back into the sterilizer.

There was a slight sound as the anaesthetist moved. He and his assistant sat at the foot of the patient, completely cut off from their colleagues behind the screen formed by the draped instrument trolleys set on either side and over the patient. While the other members of the team concentrated on the operation these two men were the sentinels of the patient's life. They watched the black oval-shaped ball attached to the anaesthetic mask as it inflated and deflated in time to the patient's breathing. At regular

intervals they took the blood-pressure and checked the pulse.

The brunette student saw the tall man next to Kirkland return his gaze to the patient's head. At the beginning of the operation the chief had scratched an outline on the shaven scalp to mark out the area where he was to operate. He had cut into the layers of skin which comprise the scalp. At this stage he had made brief, terse observations to the students who robed and masked were in the theatre.

He had drilled a hole in the skull itself to enable him to insert a very fine little saw. With this he cut away the bone. A delicate moment this, the outer layers of the skull are very hard, but the inner parts are spongy. To cut through them calls for extreme skill. Yet the chief, with his muscular hands and spatulate fingers had referred, earlier in his strong accent and with macabre humour to this part of his work as carpentry.

The white walls of the operating-theatre were high and their shining cleanliness made them look even more bare than they were. On one side ran the

row of wash-basins and taps, opposite were shelves which held large bottles of medicaments and beneath them stood trolleys on which were autoclaves, steel instrument-holders.

Everyone sensed a sudden rise of tension in the quiet, starkly clean operating-theatre. There was no hasty movement, just a slight contraction of the chief's beetling eyebrows. The critical moment had been reached. The brain had been lifted from its cavity on tapes. Now the chief had to cut away the area inside the head which was to be removed.

Almost suddenly the movements of the black ball slowed down, nearly ceased. The chief knew nothing of the patient's relapse. The anaesthetist knew. Knew the patient's life depended now on his own skill, and the chief's. He began pressing the black ball. In, out. His assistant checked the pulse.

The chief was warned of the patient's condition. He gave no sign that anything was amiss. He signalled for an instrument. The senior dresser passed it, picking it from the tray prepared by the

theatre-sister before the operation began. The chief began to cut. The theatre-sister was commenting to herself with professional pride that the chief, although she had never worked with him before, had not so far deviated from her arrangement of the lay-out of the instruments as she'd judged he'd need them.

The tall figure with the strange air of distinction about him heard the anaesthetist speak briefly to his assistant. Drugs were to be injected to sustain the patient. Slowly the black ball, which seconds before had hung like a symbol of death itself, began to move. Automatically. The breathing gradually strengthened. The patient's blood-pressure was taken. It was normal. So was his pulse.

As if he knew that the present climax had been safely passed, the tall man allowed his gaze once more to leave the operating-table. His dark, hooded eyes travelled slowly round the theatre again, seeking perhaps some relief from the impersonal, almost inhuman skill of the chief.

The brunette up in the students'

gallery wondered when she would be down there as a dresser. Three of the dressers working on this op were fourth-year students. Now she saw a staring-eyed nurse gazing fixedly at the chief's hands. Her own looked as if they were trembling. It looked like her first big operation. After this time it would never be so bad again.

Behind the glass windows of the gallery, high above the theatre floor, packed with the staring faces of students, the brunette turned to another, a man student beside her, and whispered. She had asked him if he knew who the tall figure was, he looked like someone important, didn't he agree? There was a quick nod, then both turned their eyes back to the operating-table. The nurse was still counting swabs.

The black ball moved regularly. The operation had been in progress for four hours.

As the chief worked, the tall man noticed how the joints on his powerful wrists stood out, even under the rubber gloves. How much controlled power was

there, he reflected. The part in the cavity of the head to be removed was cut away. The brain, held gently, firmly on the tapes was replaced. How strange, the brain, the tall figure ruminated. Such a delicate, wonderful piece of mechanism, so easily damaged. Yet in itself not aware of touch, only of heat.

The brunette saw the tall man press the sponge-band round his brow, tied there to absorb sweat, and while she guessed what it must be like to work in a temperature of over seventy degrees, which it had to be, she thought that the tall figure had a strangely attractive air about him, even behind the robe and mask.

It was nearly over. The anaesthetist leaned back in his chair. He grinned up at his assistant. 'He's all right, now,' he said, in a whisper, 'But there'll be no keeping this one under while the chief nips out for coffee.' He smiled at the recollection. Nobody ever believed him. But it was true. He'd held a patient under while the chief surgeon, who had been operating for eight hours, went to get a quick cup of coffee. Then the chief returned, to resume

the operation, which lasted another four hours.

The trembling ward nurse had crept closer. She took a long, steady look. Then her eyes caught those of the tall figure and she saw a glint of humour in them, as if he knew that she would feel different now, she wasn't likely to pass out now. She was over the worst. She would advance one step along the road of cool, unemotional efficiency which is the nurse's stock-in-trade.

The chief replaced the part of the skull which had been removed, then stitched back the scalp.

There was a moment of relaxed stillness. Then the chief stepped back from the table. He began to take off his rubber gloves. Turning to the students he elaborated several of the points he had made during the operation. While he talked the patient was wheeled out of the theatre. Back to the ward. Back to life.

In the students' gallery there was the unheard movement as students got up, stretched cramped limbs and began to discuss notes. The brunette student

turned away from the man who had been beside her, to watch the tall figure pull down his gauze breathing-mask and take a deep unrestricted breath. For some odd reason a thrill ran through her as she saw that he looked even more attractive than she had pictured he might be. It was a pale, aquiline face with a sardonically curved mouth above the strong chin. She wondered who he was. She asked the man next to her, and he said he thought he'd seen the face before, but couldn't place it. The girl saw the short man whom she knew to be Sir Trevor Kirkland turn to the tall man and speak to him. She wished she could hear what he said.

'Don't know about you, Dr. Morelle, but I could use some coffee,' Kirkland was saying. Dr. Morelle nodded and they went out of the operating-theatre and turned along the corridor in the direction of Sir Trevor Kirkland's office. In the office the neurologist seemed a different man. Divested of the white boots, long green gown, white linen trousers, and seen in his normal tweeds, he looked almost homely. His once-sandy hair was

sparse, his eyebrows, also sandy, were bushy. They hid keen eyes that sparkled with intelligence. The lines of his face were heavy and he was fresh-complexioned. He produced an old pipe from his pocket and began to fill it from a tobacco-tin on the mantel-piece.

A nurse brought coffee and he stirred his quickly, his pudgy fingers, a gardener's fingers, handling the spoon as delicately as if it was an artery forceps. He waved his hand at the nurse to take away the robe and trousers, boots and masks he and Dr. Morelle had discarded.

Dr. Morelle wore a dark grey worsted single-breasted suit and a dark bow tie; an inch of silk shirt cuff showed at his sleeves.

Kirkland indicated the bowl of roses that stood on the table. 'Aren't they fine? Cut them myself this morning, before I left home. Yesterday morning, I should say,' he glanced at his watch which showed one-thirty a.m. 'It's a good year for roses. Mine have never been better.' He waved his spoon in the direction of the operation-theatre. 'What did you think of it?'

'The new techniques he demonstrated were remarkably impressive.' Dr. Morelle said.

The other nodded enthusiastically and plunged into a technical résumé of what had transpired on the operation-table, ending up by asking Dr. Morelle if he would like to join him in a discussion with the surgeon himself. But Dr. Morelle declined politely, explaining that he was leaving early for the South of France.

'I heard you were going,' Kirkland said. He opened the hand-finished silver cigarette-box on his desk and offered it to Dr. Morelle.

'I will smoke my own, if you don't mind.' And Dr. Morelle took out and lit a Le Sphinx. Smoke curled up as the two men talked. Sir Trevor questioned Dr. Morelle about his forthcoming trip. He expressed envy that Dr. Morelle should have had a villa in Monte Carlo lent to him so opportunely.

Dr. Morelle nodded. 'It is fortunate. I was beginning to find it difficult to obtain the peace I need, in London. Like you, I suffer from too many consultations.'

'I thought the famous Miss Frayle guarded your privacy,' the other said humorously.

A faint frown contracted Dr. Morelle's eyebrows. He said coldly, 'Miss Frayle left my employ some time ago. She wished to widen her experience and education. She is studying at the Sorbonne.'

'Miss Frayle in Paris, eh? Is she enjoying it?'

'I believe so.' Dr. Morelle turned away. He appeared to be studying the roses in the bowl. Then Kirkland saw his glance drift to the clock on the office wall and he made a movement towards the door. 'Must you go? I hoped you might have time for a talk with his nibs.'

'I'm afraid not,' Dr. Morelle said. 'I have to pack for the plane.'

The two men walked to the door. As Dr. Morelle went off down the corridor, Sir Trevor called after him, wishing him a comfortable trip, but Dr. Morelle didn't seem to hear him. He didn't turn back.

2

Despite the warmth of the day the room was cool and restful. Bookshelves flanked one side of it, encasing a library of medical works. There was nothing clinical about the room, only the heavy folding screen and the surgical couch indicated its true purpose. The deep Persian carpet harmonized with the plain comfortable furniture and the rich draperies of the large window. A bowl of roses stood on the oak gate-legged table. Sunlight streaming through the window slanted across the big mahogany desk, glowing on the antique surface of the wood.

Sir Trevor Kirkland had been writing his notes and now he pushed back the swivel chair to avoid the strong sunlight. He relaxed his elbows on the arms of the chair and clasped his short-fingered pudgy hands together. There was little about his hands to indicate his profession, except the extreme cleanliness of the

nails. He stared thoughtfully at the screen across the room, behind which his patient was dressing. His face was unlined, as fresh and untroubled as a countryman's.

Ian Laking straightened the knot of his tie and slipped into his Savile Row jacket. Instead of coming out from behind the screen he stood staring at his reflection in the oval mirror. He saw a once-handsome face, a face with the flesh drawn tightly over the cheekbones, there were dark hollows under the eyes. His hair was as thick and dark as it had always been, but there was more grey at the temples.

He stared at himself in the glass, stared into his dark, curiously lifeless eyes. With a conscious effort he stepped out from behind the screen into the pool of sunlight flooding the room. He didn't feel the warmth of the sunshine, didn't sense the sympathy the other man was extending to him.

Kirkland indicated the leather armchair in front of his desk. Laking sat down. He said nothing, just waited, watching. Sir Trevor looked down at his notes. He had already made up his mind

who could best treat Laking, and it appeared the arrangement would work out very well. He fixed his gaze on Laking's face.

'I want to assure you, Mr. Laking, that my thorough examination of you reveals absolutely nothing physically wrong with you. The X-ray plates showed nothing, and I have satisfied myself there is no organic disease. Every bodily function is working normally.' He leaned forward, said deliberately, 'It is the state of your mind which causes the distress. You should undergo a course of psychiatric treatment.'

'Is it really necessary?' Laking said harshly.

'Not only necessary, but urgent. The treatment should start immediately.'

'Then I can't go back to Monte Carlo?' The question came quickly.

Kirkland relaxed in his chair, smiling slightly. 'On the contrary, you should go back at once. The specialist I wish you to see happens to be staying at Monte Carlo. He is doing some work there, quietly, but he will, I know, on hearing from me, be

pleased to help you.' His mind went back to the operating theatre in the early hours of that morning three days ago, and then the brief chat over coffee, afterwards, with the tall, gaunt figure.

'Who is he?'

'Dr. Morelle.' Sir Trevor picked up his pen and began writing on a sheet of notepaper. 'You may have heard of him,' he said without raising his head.

'I have.' Laking sounded surprised, his expression was suddenly wary.

'Dr. Morelle's criminological work forms only a small part of his activities,' Kikland said. 'Shall we say the more sensational part that gets into the papers?'

'You think he'd be willing to treat me, out there?' The other sounded dubious.

'I have no doubt that he will appreciate the urgency of your case. How long are you staying there?'

'I've taken the villa for three months,' Laking said. 'We've been there two weeks.'

'We? Mrs. Laking is with you?'

'Yes. Also my secretary.'

'So you are able to avoid any business worries?'

Laking hesitated, but only for a moment. 'I pay people to do the worrying for me,' he said brusquely. 'My secretary and my right-hand man.'

'Then there appears to be no obstacle in the way of your taking a course of treatment,' the surgeon said. 'I cannot say what Dr. Morelle will advise, but you should see him as soon as you return.'

'I'm returning on the early afternoon flight,' Laking said.

Sir Trevor nodded. 'I will write to Dr. Morelle at once and explain the position fully. Meantime, will you take this introductory note along. I have put his address on the envelope.'

He folded the letter, slipped it into the envelope and sealed it. He came round the desk and handed the envelope to Laking. He pressed a buzzer and his receptionist entered. The two men shook hands and then Laking was being shown out into the hot midday sunshine of Harley Street.

Laking walked up Harley Street to the corner of New Cavendish Street. He lit a cigarette, wondered if the girl who

glanced at him as she passed could see his hand tremble. Dragging nervously at his cigarette he walked along New Cavendish Street and turned into Portland Place.

He crossed the wide thoroughfare to the terrace of Regency houses on the further side. He walked quickly, glancing neither right nor left and turned into Layton Street. There, almost facing him, was the business he had built, built from one best-selling book.

He went through the reception office with an absent nod at the girl behind the desk, and upstairs to his lavishly equipped front office on the first floor. His desk and trays were clear, the bookshelves tidy, bookshelves lined with books bearing the imprint of the House of Laking on their spines.

Laking didn't notice them, nor how the polished furniture shone in the sunlight. He went straight to the plain cabinet against the wall. He unlocked it, took out a whisky-bottle and poured himself a stiff shot, squirted in a dash of soda and swallowed it at a gulp. He poured another, stood it on top of the cabinet on

the ornate metal tray. He returned the bottle and siphon and locked the cabinet door.

He sat down at the desk, picked up the ivory paper knife, twisting the blade between his twitching fingers. He wasn't looking forward to going back to Monte Carlo. Consult Dr. Morelle? That was a laugh. His mind was ill? Kirkland had said it, and that was a laugh, too. His body was fine. He smiled to himself. It wasn't a genial smile.

He took another gulp from the glass as the knock came on the door. He was lighting a cigarette when Dyke Fenton's secretary came in. She was a tall, slim girl. She wore a pleated black skirt and a soft white shirt fastened with a black bow at the neck. She was always calm and efficient but she had the eyes of a flirt. Only she never flirted with her employers.

'I heard you come in,' she said, stepping into the room. 'This cable from New York, about one of the manuscripts Mr. Fenton took away with him.' she held out the cable. 'Do you want to send him any instructions?'

'Leave the cable,' Laking said. 'I'll ring for you in a few minutes.'

The girl went out. Laking stared at the cable on his pad. He was seeing Dyke Fenton clearly in his mind. Fenton was a good type. Bachelor. Keen business-sense and a nose for best-sellers.

Laking stared at the book in its place of honour in the special bookcase. *The Life And Times Of Harry Laking*. Ian Laking's father. The old man's face glared out at him from the dust jacket. It seemed to mock him and the business he had built on it. More, his father's face was condemning him, so that as always he had to turn away from it. Laking had never found a really worthwhile book since then. But Fenton had. Fenton got on well with people. With Laking himself. And with Stacey. And Sara, she liked him too. Fenton must feel good. The boss's wife, the secretary and the boss himself, all in the palm of his hand.

Fenton was a good mixer. Easy-going, but underneath it a great capacity for business, for doing the right thing. He never looked out of place anywhere. He

21

wouldn't look out of place in Monte Carlo, where he was right now.

Laking pressed the bell-push on the desk. The idea was stronger now, the outlines clearer. The consultation with Kirkland hadn't worked out quite as he'd thought it would, but it was going to be all right.

Fenton's secretary came in again and stood waiting, while Laking tried to remember what it was he wanted to tell her about, the other business was so much on his mind.

3

Laking dreaded it, that unpleasant queasy feeling in the pit of the stomach whenever the plane left the runway. He had flown often enough but it made no difference. Always that strange disembodied feeling as the aircraft lifted against the pull of gravity. He had to avert his eyes from the windows until the blurred sweep of the ground rushing past just below became a flat, unmoving map thousands of feet away.

He had decided to get the Air France Riviera Express, from London Airport direct to Nice. He would be back in Monte Carlo soon after four that afternoon. He didn't mind the actual flight. Air travel was quick, comfortable and there was no fuss. Once in the air there was hardly any sensation of flying at all. When the great triangle of runways receded and he could unfasten his seat belt and smoke, the tension and sickness

vanished and he could relax.

The faint hum of the four Rolls Royce Dart engines was hardly noticeable in the large pressurized cabin. It was hard to believe that this great turbo-prop monster, eighty-one feet long, its wingspan ninety-four feet, was cruising twenty-thousand feet up, flying towards France at three hundred and ten miles per hour. The smoothness of the flight, the attentive service of the stewards and hostess filled Laking with pleasure.

It was one of his peculiarities that he must always understand the principles of any machine in whose care he had put himself. Cars, ships, aircraft, he had to know how they were driven. Although under their cowlings these aircraft engines appeared huge and complicated, he knew the principle on which they worked was one of the simplest, known and applied since earliest times.

The familiar water-wheel, still seen in rural districts, was itself a turbine, by replacing its paddles with a double ring of high-speed steel blades, and the mill-stream by a powerful jet of gas produced

by burning heavy fuel in compressed air, the modern turbine had evolved. The only difference in the latest turbines, Laking knew, was that they made use of gas expansion, giving them greater efficiency than the earlier ones, the compressed air being supplied by compressors driven by the turbine itself, and started up electrically.

The cabin was spacious, elegantly upholstered in beige. There was a complete absence of noise and vibration. Laking lounged back in one of the forty-nine adjustable arm-chairs and waited for the attractive French hostess to bring his luncheon tray.

Laking took a whisky and soda with his meal. He had little appetite for the appetizing concoction despite its traditional French delicacy. He picked at the food, envying the dark bearded Indian next to him who ate with noisy ravenous appetite.

The passengers were a mixed bunch. The Indian spent the flight with his nose buried in law books. The obvious Californian business-man across the aisle

spent most of the flight drinking champagne and chewing a fat cigar. At intervals he dictated to an ash-blonde secretary who lazily caressed the keys of a portable typewriter on the table fitted to the front of her seat. There was a family of six forward, holiday-bound, with four noisy young children the hostess did her best to amuse with an assortment of games. There was a man shuffling cards and laying them out for solitaire, game after game. Next to him his wife sat engrossed in a fashion magazine. But most of the passengers lay back, eyes closed, enjoying an after-lunch doze.

Laking finished his whisky and squashed his cigarette into the ash-tray. He leaned back, his mind jumping ahead to Monte Carlo. There would be no-one at the airport to meet him. He didn't expect anyone. Stacey had no interest in him. She'd be out somewhere, with friends. Or with Dyke Fenton.

Laking's thoughts slipped into the old groove. Fenton was his editorial director. He had joined him as general editor soon after the company had been formed, and

his hard work and efficiency had soon won him a directorship. Laking relied on him and over the years Fenton had become more than just a colleague, he had become a friend. Now, looking back, Laking realized Fenton had become too friendly. Especially with Stacey.

Stacey had persuaded him to take the Villa des Fleurs again for the season. It had followed Fenton should occupy the small bachelor apartment nearby as he had done the year before. Sara Belling was there too, staying in the villa with Stacey and himself. Sara would always be there, the perfect secretary.

It was as if Laking had transferred his business from London to flourish in the sun of the South. And it had flourished. His uncertainty, when Stacey had first mooted the idea, had quickly been dispelled. Business routine continued uninterrupted and the short air journeys that either he or Fenton had undertaken between London and Monte Carlo had been necessary only on rare occasions.

The villa at Monte Carlo was the ideal setting for the drama he was planning.

The drama of which his visit to Kirkland had been the first act.

Laking was jerked out of his reverie. The hostess handed him the customs and police forms. To fill them in now, she said, saved time when they landed. Nice was now less than thirty minutes flying time away. Laking completed the forms and by the time the hostess had collected them the warning notice 'Fasten Your Seat Belts' flashed on the panel and they were descending towards the Côte d'Azur Airport.

Laking passed through the French landing formalities in quick time. In less than half an hour he was on his way in a private hire car to Monte Carlo. He savoured the luxuriousness of the limousine. He appreciated warmth and luxury, always had done, ever since his first taste of expensive living. Ever since he had left his meagre existence, stepped into big business through that one stroke of good fortune. He had hoped never to look back, but it hadn't worked out that way. Not quite. He frowned, and stared out of the car-window.

Nothing could ever take away his memories of the Côte d'Azur. He knew the coast from Marseilles to the Italian frontier, the villages and towns of Provence, the land of olive trees. This whole stretch of the Mediterranean was as familiar to him as the streets of London.

Here on the Côte d'Azur the sun shone all year, semitropical plants — palms, lemons, bananas, prickly-pears — flourished in the warm sea-scented breezes. Here life was full of carnival, battles of flowers, motor rallies, *concours d'elegance* followed each other in brilliant succession. On a hundred golden beaches brown-bodied men and women played around, film-stars, celebrities, holiday-makers, from all over the world.

Laking had travelled the coast road many times from Marseilles to Menton near the frontier. He had visited the Calanques of Cassis, the Baie des Anges, the Baie de la Napoule and the tiny coves of Le Trayas, cut in the red rock of the Esterel. He had wandered in the brightly-coloured ports of Villefranche and St.

Tropez, frequented by artists. He knew too the fashionable resorts — Juan les Pins, Cannes itself, a town as elegant as the yachts that come from all over the world to shelter in its harbour.

In those early seasons he and Stacey had driven to the flowering fields of Grasse. Stacey had collected samples of the perfumes made there. They had marvelled at the wild gorges of Le Cians and Dalius, and from a road cut out of the living rock they had looked out over the vast canyon of the Verdon. But most of all, from those first trips, he remembered Provence and long summer days full of the scent of thyme and lavender and the music of the cigales.

Provence had been like a page from a history of art with its relics from former ages carefully preserved, some dating from Roman times. How much more memorable it had been with Stacey at his side. The arena, the Maison Caree of Nimes, the Aqueduct of Pont du Gard, the triumphal arch and the Roman theatre of Orange, the antiques of St. Remy. The Roman remains at Arles, the

theatre, the arena, the Alyscamps, and the church of St. Trophime whose gateway was a masterpiece of Romanesque architecture.

Memories whirled in his brain, sun-filled, dazzling, all of them flavoured with the scent of Stacey's hair, the brownness of her skin, her excited laugh. Meals in softly-lighted inns and restaurants, piquant and appetizing food gently seasoned with garlic, olive-oil and spices, heady with the Rhône wines, Château Neuf-du-Pape and Tavel. He remembered their first sight of the glittering Promenade des Anglais at Nice, their exploration of the Principality of Monaco with its Palais Oceanographique and its subtropical gardens and the famous Monte Carlo itself. And now here they were, renting a villa for the second year.

But no longer alone. Nothing was the same. Nothing could be the same again; until, Laking's face was grim, until his plan had run its course.

He paid off the car at the foot of the steps. Taking the light valise and the briefcase he slowly climbed the slope to the steps that ran alongside the white

two-storey villa. Once above the neatly laid out garden with its shrubs and palms he turned to take in the view above the green tiles of his roof.

In the brilliant afternoon sunshine the sea was a smooth expanse of lapis-lazuli fringed with a white strip of sand and the stone of the promenade wall. The town clustered down to the water's edge and at the further end he could see the inlet to the tiny harbour. Behind, towering on the great rock was the Palace of Monaco.

Laking's gaze came slowly back to his own villa. Through the screen of shrubs he could see the open french windows of the library. The white paved terrace ran the whole length of the villa. It was separated from the lawn by orange trees and clusters of mimosa. Green shutters lay back against the white walls on either side of the window and small balconies opened out from two of the bedrooms with balustrades of decorated wrought-iron.

Laking walked back down the slope and went down the steps alongside the garden to the wide iron gates between a

pair of orange trees. Before going in he looked back up the broad walk which led to the road above. The white façades of detached villas dazzled his eyes in the strong sunlight. The soft greens and reds of shrubs and flowers and trees were etched vividly against the brilliant blue of the sky. His gaze wandered further. To the flat roof of the apartment block. An attractive building, three storeys high.

Laking could just make out the top floor through the palm fronds which decorated the lush, shady garden. Fenton rented an apartment on the second floor. Laking wondered if he was there, working. He liked to think so, but he went on wondering.

He turned and pushed open the gate, descending the wide gravel steps to the terrace. He went quietly along it to the terrace and paused by the french windows.

There was the soft clicking of an almost silent typewriter. A girl sat at his desk, her back turned to him. The suntanned arms revealed by the sleeveless nylon blouse hardly moved as her fingers flicked over

the keys. Her hair was dark, cut short over the nape of the neck. She wore a gay summer skirt, fastened at the waist with a wide silver-link belt.

Laking surveyed her for a long moment then the clicking ceased and she turned abruptly. Her face was small, oval, her cheek-bones high and pronounced. He noted the firm mouth and the intense blue of her eyes as for a second they stared at each other.

She got up gracefully from the desk. 'Why, Ian,' she said. 'I didn't hear you.'

'Hello, Sara,' Laking said, and entered the room.

4

Sara Belling took Laking's briefcase, placing it on the low refectory table alongside the cream wall. She crossed to the desk and gathered up papers, a file and the typewriter.

Laking let his valise drop on the turquoise carpet and threw his hat into a chair. 'Where's Stacey?' he said.

'She went out before lunch.' Sara clutched her belongings. 'I've been working in here while you've been away. It's cool. And that view from the front of the house is fatal. I could spend hours looking across the bay. I'll take these up to my room.' She paused in front of the desk. 'You hungry? I could make some tea.'

'I had lunch on the plane. Right now I want a bath and a change.' His eyes were weary.

'Okay.' Sarah went out and Laking stood still, gazing round the room. It was

a pleasant room. Large, light and cool with comfortable, unostentatious furnishings. The cream and turquoise décor was kind to the eyes after a spell in the sun's glare. There were dark oak bookcases with sliding glass panels. A glass chandelier hung from the centre of the carved ceiling and there were wrought-iron bracket lights round the walls. The fireplace was almost hidden by a Japanese screen and the fronds of palm set in a copper vase in front of it. A big settee, gaily cushioned, on one side of the french windows and a chaise-longue opposite. The desk was plain old oak, wide and roomy with deep drawers.

Laking liked the room. It was the room in which his plan would be fulfilled.

He crossed the room and looked at himself in the Adam mirror. He saw the same reflection which had stared out from Kirkland's mirror in London. He smiled grimly.

He swung round to the citrus-wood cabinet and opened the top exposing an array of decanters and glasses. He collected his hat and valise and went into

the hall and up the wide staircase.

The library reflected Laking's own tastes, but once outside it the more rococo tastes of the man who had commissioned this villa became apparent. A Birmingham manufacturer, Laking reflected dryly, patting one of the naked statues familiarly as he passed. The man had gratified his desire to have nudes about him in the most permanent fashion. They dotted the garden, these nude statues, some peeped coyly out from the shrubbery which surrounded the front part of the house. Inside the entrance hall there were more of them, the two largest standing demurely on either side of the vast staircase.

Next to the library was a *salon* and next to that a dining-room which was entered by double doors under the archway formed by the stairs. The windows of the dining-room overlooked the terrace. On the other side of the dining-room were archways, through which could be seen a staircase up to a gallery. The bedrooms could be reached from this staircase as from the main

staircase in the entrance hall.

Opposite the library there was a smoking-room and a drawing-room. From this side of the house terraced lawns looked directly over Monte Carlo and straight across the bay to Italy.

There were three bedrooms on the first floor, also a tiled bathroom fitted with an elaborate partially-sunk bath and a shower. The front bedrooms had windows opening on to narrow high-railed balconies and the tall landing window opened on to the flat roof of the portico. The view of the bay from these windows was magnificent.

Laking bathed and slipped into a cream silk shirt and light drill trousers. He was careful to set his bow tie straight before putting on a light jacket. Then he went down to the library and he was sitting at his desk when Sara came in. She carried a dish of crystallized fruits. She placed them on the desk. Laking looked up. 'Anything happen while I was away?'

She shook her head. 'Nothing important. I've been dealing with the routine

correspondence under Dyke's instructions.'

Laking nodded, lifting his briefcase on to the desk. 'I called at the office before I left this morning,' he said. 'Brought one or two things away. We'll get down to work tomorrow.'

'Just one thing,' Sara said suddenly. 'Dyke is really excited about the manuscript. Says it's a real find. He telephoned about half-an-hour before you got here. He'd like to talk to you about it as soon as possible.'

'Yes. I want to see him.' Laking's voice was quiet. 'Give him a ring. Tell him to come over early this evening for a drink.'

'I'll do it now.' She hesitated, glancing at him. 'You sure there's nothing more I can get you?'

He began taking papers from his case. 'There'll be nothing else.'

They exchanged glances. Sara smiled at him, then she went out closing the door quietly behind her. Laking sat staring at the door until the sound of her high-heeled shoes on the parquet floor of the hall ceased. She would telephone

from her room. He pushed his briefcase aside, took a sheet of note-paper from the top drawer of the desk. He began to write a letter.

Slowly, carefully the thoughts dribbled from his mind The words looked strange to him now, on the white paper. It was a long time before he finished. When he had signed his name he read the letter through. Then slowly again. Satisfied, he wrote out the envelope, folded the letter, inserted it and sealed the flap. He stared at the address he had written.

A bleak smile touched his lips. It was all too easy. He was going to be the innocent party. The unsuspecting villain of the piece would never be able to extricate himself from this.

The letter must be posted at once, then he must get back and prepare for the trickiest part, which was yet to come. He would have to be careful. Dyke Fenton was an astute character, not easily fooled. He must be led gently, convinced beyond any shadow of doubt. Dyke knew he had gone to London specially to see Kirkland. That visit was part of the plan. It would

help make Dyke Fenton swallow the act.

Laking slipped the letter in his pocket and went out into the hall. He called up to Sara and she came to the top of the stairs.

'What time is Dyke coming?'

'He said six o'clock,' Sara said.

Laking nodded. 'I'm going out but I'll be back before that.' He let himself out of the front door.

He hurried down the wide steps. As he walked down the hill he looked back at the villa, looked up at the windows. But Sara's small oval face was not there, watching.

Lower down the hill the road turned and he had a view of the sea between white buildings. He found the pillar box and he pushed the letter into the box, heard it plop on to the heap inside. Then he lit a cigarette and gazed idly along the street. A few people passed in the sunshine but Laking eyed them without curiosity.

As he moved away he glanced back, there was a squeaking of bicycle brakes and a uniformed postman had pulled up

in front of the pillar box.

Laking paused and watched the post-man open the box and shovel the letters into his bag. His eyes followed the uniformed figure down the road until he was lost from view.

5

The Villa Midnight stood on high wooded ground at the eastern end of Monte Carlo. It was set in extensive gardens which lay behind high white walls, and the entrance was through tall ornamental gates. The house was secluded, islanded in a sea of blossom. In the brilliant sun the white walls of the garden shimmered, reflecting the rich purple of the heliotropes which were banked along it.

Throughout the year flowers blazed in the garden, white mimosa, anemones, marigolds, cyclamen, carnations, geraniums, flowers of every possible colour. Only the vivid, succulent-looking oranges and tangerines which grew in the centre of the garden were a delusion, for they were acid and bitter to the taste. The spectacular Indian-rubber trees and palms which were set round the garden gave a subtropical beauty to the surroundings.

The villa, like most in the vicinity, was

white. It was not a large residence but it had all the comforts and luxuries of a villa set in a Mediterranean setting. The Comtesse saw to that. An open portico in the front of the house led to the main door. The amazingly big entrance hall had a table in the centre and its rose-coloured walls stretched the full height of the house. Straight ahead was a beautiful hand-carved staircase which led up to a gallery from which the bedrooms could be reached. Each of the bedrooms had a private bathroom. The sunken baths were coloured to match the tones used in the bedrooms.

Most of the rooms on the ground floor had plain white panelled walls. The morning-room was to the left of the main door and was furnished with a fine collection of Veronese antiques. Next to that was an entrance leading to the kitchen and servants' quarters. Opposite the morning-room was a studio in which the Comtesse occasionally spent some time. She was a talented artist, and this was the room of which she was most proud. Venetian crystal lights threw a soft

glow upwards to the painted ceiling. The furniture was Louis XV and over the mantelpiece was an old Venetian mirror which looked like a gem, and shone with all the brilliance of one.

Exquisite hand-painted frescoes everywhere were the envy of everyone who visited the villa. The library in particular had a magnificent display of murals. This room was entered by a door under the balcony. It was the library which Dr. Morelle used. Two walls of the library were covered in books and the fine old desk was Italian, as were the chairs.

The library opened on to a colonnaded veranda which ran the full length of the back of the house. The veranda overlooked an Italian garden and from it there was a magnificent view of the mountainous Riviera coastline leading to Italy. The wooded slopes of the Alpes Maritimes stretched away from the front of the house.

Somewhere behind the villa a motor-mower puttered its way across the lawn. A faint unobtrusive sound that failed to interrupt the peace of the gardens or the

concentration of the occupant of the terrace.

Presently the gaunt figure in the wicker chair paused and put down his pen, pushing the foolscap sheets of manuscript away from him across the coffee table. He glanced along the terrace as he heard footsteps.

A dumpy woman in a black dress offset by a white lace apron appeared and came diffidently forward. 'If there will be nothing more, m'sieu. I will take my leave.' She spoke in excellent English but with a strong French accent. 'I have laid out everything for your dinner as usual.'

Dr. Morelle took a Le Sphinx from the box on the table. His sombre face relaxed in a smile. 'I am sure you have arranged everything for my comfort with your usual efficiency.'

'*Merci, m'sieu.*' The woman moved away quickly and disappeared into the house. Dr. Morelle noticed that the sound of the mower had ceased and a few minutes later the gardener appeared. He glanced up at the terrace and went off down the drive. Soon afterwards the

dumpy woman followed him, a light coat over her severe dress, and a basket in her hand.

Dr. Morelle would have preferred unbroken solitude, but the Comtesse had insisted he have the attention of her servants for at least a few hours each day. So it had been arranged that the housekeeper and her husband arrived early each morning and left again in the afternoon. Dr. Morelle had to admit he hardly knew of their presence, so unobtrusive were they. The work upon which he was engaged took his undivided attention and he had felt that the presence of someone in the house, however silent, would disturb him.

The Comtesse was a beautiful woman, a persuasive woman. It had been difficult to refuse her generous offer of the villa while she was in America. It was a debt of gratitude, she insisted, for Dr. Morelle's brilliant success in rescuing her from a somewhat menacing situation which she had found herself in some little while ago. The Comtesse's gratitude had been quite overwhelming. Dr. Morelle smiled a trifle

sardonically to himself at the thought.

He had contrived to keep her at arm's length but when they had met at a party in London a few weeks ago and he had mentioned his intention of working for a month somewhere in the sun, she had immediately offered him the Villa Midnight overlooking Monte Carlo. She was off to America and meanwhile her villa would be standing empty, and she did not like that. What better opportunity for her to return the favour? If Dr. Morelle would work there she would feel not only had she been of some service, but she might also take a little credit for the great work he would accomplish beneath the elegant roof of the Villa Midnight.

She had been so insistent, it would have been ungracious to refuse her. So the arrangements had been made and he had come to Monte Carlo and the Villa Midnight.

He had allowed himself a month to complete the work, no more, for work would be accumulating at his house in Harley Street and now Miss Frayle was no longer there to attend to the

day-to-day routine he did not look forward to the mass of routine work which would face him on his return.

Dr. Morelle picked a letter from his table. It bore a Paris postmark and was written in a not entirely unfamiliar scrawl.

Dr. Morelle had missed Miss Frayle, though he would have admitted it to no-one. For several months he had suffered the attentions of a succession of secretaries, who had emphasized the gap in his social and professional life Miss Frayle's departure for Paris had caused. But there was nothing to be done about it. If Miss Frayle wished to be independent of him he would never consider any attempt to change her mind.

He re-read snatches of her letter, that faint sardonic smile flickering across his face. Undoubtedly Miss Frayle was also missing him. Did he detect a hint that she would like to return to his employ? Was there also a suggestion that she might be coming to Monte Carlo? He sighed. It would be a further interruption to the quiet schedule he had set himself, but her services would undeniably be useful.

Dr. Morelle stubbed his cigarette into the ash-tray and got up from his chair. He stared out through the palm fronds to the sea, his eyes dark and hooded. The sea looked warm, inviting, with sunlight flecking the blue with a myriad scintillating diamonds as a freshening breeze stirred the surface. Two yachts sailed close in company back to the harbour, white canvas taut, their lee rails under a bubbling cascade of foam.

Dr. Morelle turned abruptly. The Mediterranean was a seductive mistress and to linger in admiration of her beauty was fatal when there was work to be done. He gathered up his papers, thrust the two letters into his pocket, his thoughts as he entered the villa returning to Miss Frayle.

6

Miss Frayle hadn't really meant to buy the Samurai sword.

Afterwards, in the train heading for the South, she could attribute it only to a combination of over-excitement an inflated sense of her own bargaining powers and the general noise and confusion of the Paris Flea Market.

She had been set on going there ever since her arrival in Paris. That it had taken her so many months to achieve her ambition she put down to the stuffiness of Madame Grimault, in whose apartment she had rented a room. Madame Grimault had frowned and raised her hands in dismay every time Miss Frayle suggested an outing. Either the season was wrong, or the time of day, or the place was too touristy, it would be vulgar to be seen gaping at it. Unwilling to offend her, Miss Frayle always gave in. But nothing would keep her from visiting

the famous Flea Market. If need be, she would go alone.

She had gone alone. Cheeks pink with excitement, eyes gleaming behind her horn-rims, she left the Metro at Porte de Clignancourt and looked about her for the market. What she saw had made her gasp. At a wide junction where several boulevards met was what appeared like a flattened bomb site on which stood rows of stalls. She felt indignant. Flea Market, she thought. Looks more like a moth-eaten Petticoat Lane.

She walked through the Marché Biron, the Marché Vernaison and the Cité Paul Bert. As she did so her first disappointment had begun to give away to excitement. Before her was a ghetto of streets and passageways, all crammed with treasure. Tiny shops and junk-laden stalls overflowed out of the narrow streets. Some vendors had spread blankets on the pavements, too poor to show their wares on stalls. Miss Frayle had been told there were about three thousand shops in the market. There seemed to be far more.

The market was jammed with people,

sharp-eyed French housewives, tourists from all over the world, students, giggling girls, dealers. It was the dealers, she knew, who had made the market what it was to-day. It had started at the end of the last century when the rag-pickers who still search the dustbins of Paris every morning made their headquarters near the northern walls of the city. Miss Frayle had learned how they began the market and it was their reputation for being verminous which had gained it the name Marché aux Puces.

At the turn of the century tourists had discovered the place and begun to find amusement in observing the strange collection of rubbish on the stalls. It was not long before Paris antique dealers heard of it and they were swift to realize the potential value of the market. They began to rent lots there.

Nowadays, prosperous shopkeepers displayed fine wares, furniture, china, crystal, sometimes even an Old Master, Miss Frayle had been told, and many of the most expensive Paris shops kept branches in the Marché aux Puces.

Miss Frayle wandered from stall to stall, completely fascinated by the wild assortment of merchandise. Stall-holders shouted or cajoled. Here were fantastic bargains, they assured her. An ivory fan, a superb brass bedstead, a set of motor-car tyres, good as new, a stuffed owl in a cage. Miss Frayle got tired of shaking her head, murmuring: '*Non merci,*' or: '*Pas aujourd'hui.*' A small lank-haired man in a greasy gaberdine jabbed at her with a dirty finger as she passed. '*Vous manquez une parapluie, M'selle?*' he leered. He stared hopefully at the brilliant blue sky. '*Le ciel va tomber.*'

Colour rushed into Miss Frayle's face. 'Oh,' she said, outraged. 'You horrid little man.' And she marched quickly away leaving him staring after her in bewilderment.

Umbrellas had a special meaning for Miss Frayle. When she had arrived in Paris she was warned it would be difficult to find accommodation. She soon found how true it was. She searched for a week but every cheap hotel she tried turned her away as soon as they heard she would be

staying in Paris for a year. For, as she had found out, lower-class hotels are controlled by law and have to charge a price much lower than the daily rate for anyone staying longer than a month.

Miss Frayle had been desperate. She visited the students' advisory office at the Sorbonne but when the two women sitting behind the counter heard what she wanted they hooted with laughter. 'All the rooms on our books were taken months ago,' one woman said, staring at Miss Frayle as if she were an imbecile. She returned miserably to her hotel where she was paying eight hundred francs a day simply for a room, without food. She would have to find a room for herself, she decided.

The next day she had set out. She left the Metro at the Odeon, walked along the Boulevard St. Germain and then turned towards Pont Neuf. She bought some cheap grapes in a little market and picked her way through the twisting little streets until she came to a narrow passageway, where she saw a small hotel.

It was a perfect setting, she thought

enthusiastically. This was the Paris she had read about, little winding streets with buildings that must date back to the Revolution, and a colourful market round the corner. At one end of the cobbled passageway there was a café, next to it an *épicerie*. On the opposite corner a laundry. Blinking through the doorway, Miss Frayle had thought of Zola's *L'Assommoir*.

A small boy ran past her pushing a hoop which bobbled and banged over the cobbles. This, thought Miss Frayle, is Paris. Without hesitation she marched into the hotel. The concierge was a little round woman who would have been improved by a visit to the laundry on the corner. Her hair was a grey bird's nest and it seemed to tremble even more wispily when Miss Frayle asked for accommodation. She gaped at this sedate-looking girl. Then she pursed her lips as if about to say: '*Non.*' But Miss Frayle looked at her so imploringly that the woman shrugged and led the way up a dark, narrow staircase to a room on the first floor.

A girl carrying a pencil-thin umbrella passed them on the landing. Much too blonde and over-dressed, Miss Frayle had decided disapprovingly. And I don't much like the look of her boyfriend. Decidedly greasy. The conceirge showed her into the room. It was small and sparsely furnished. There was a bed against the far wall, a wardrobe behind the door. A wobbly table stood in the middle of the room and there was a chest of drawers by the window. Miss Frayle was not dismayed. She observed that the room was clean and that the wash-basin had two taps, which promised hot water. 'How much?' she asked.

'Four-hundred-and-fifty francs a day,' the woman told her.

'Can I use my oil-stove to cook in here?'

The woman shrugged. 'You can do what you like, it makes no difference to me, just so long as you pay the rent.'

'How long can I stay?' asked Miss Frayle hesitantly, expecting to have her hopes dashed.

'Just so long as you pay the rent.' Indifferently.

'More than a month? But what about — ?'

'I said as long as you like,' the woman interrupted. 'If the law is broken that's your business. I just want my money.'

Miss Frayle had blinked. A law-breaker? What would Dr. Morelle think? However she was eager to take the room and the bargain was struck. She had moved in the next day, feeling highly elated. That night she went to bed early and fell asleep calculating how much she would save on rent and how she could economize by being able to cook her own food.

She had awoken suddenly. It was dark. She heard the sound of two people clumping up the stairs. They went up to the next floor and a door banged. A few minutes later a door on her own landing opened and she heard two people walk down the stairs and out into the street. Miss Frayle had dozed off. About half-an-hour later there were more footsteps on the stairs and the door of the

adjoining room opened and shut. Miss Frayle put her head under the blankets but by now a regular traffic had started up and down the stairs.

She had sat up in bed with a weary sigh, wondering what on earth was happening. Sleep was impossible. She tried to read but she could not even settle to her book. Five minutes later there had sounded a tap on her own door.

Miss Frayle gave a frightened gasp. Who could it be? No one knew she lived here. She was about to get out of her bed to answer the door when there was another tap. An urgent male voice had whispered: 'Mademoiselle, mademoiselle.'

Miss Frayle dived under the bed clothes and remained there quaking long after the friendly stranger had stopped trying to persuade her it would be fun if she would open the door to him. Emerging at last hot-faced from the blankets, Miss Frayle decided to complain to the concierge in the morning. However the first light of day comforted her and she soon fell asleep. When she awoke she rebuked herself for being

hysterical and decided to say nothing.

At lunchtime when she arrived home from the morning lectures at the Sorbonne, Miss Frayle saw the over-blonde blonde again. This time she was with two other gaudily-dressed girls. There was no sign of rain, yet all three carried long thin umbrellas. And that evening Miss Frayle saw them again, standing on the corner of the passageway, umbrellas still in evidence. A man approached one of the girls. There was a short, sharp conversation, then the girl nodded amicably and the man followed her into the hotel.

Miss Frayle had felt herself turn scarlet. She turned away blinking through her spectacles, and then she had jumped as a hand touched her arm. 'How dare you,' she started, but it was the concierge.

'*Bonsoir, Mademoiselle*. Are you coming in?'

Angry words rose to Miss Frayle's lips, then she thought helplessly she must sleep somewhere, and had followed the woman dumbly back to the hotel. As they entered three more girls came out. It was obvious enough what they were. Miss

Frayle averted her eyes. Umbrellas, she had thought, as she walked nervously up to her room, must be their hallmark.

That night Miss Frayle pushed the chest of drawers up against her door. She had lain in bed listening to the noises. To make matters even more frightening, three men, all of them residents in the hotel, had in turn knocked hopefully at her door. She was thankful to have barred the entrance.

By six in the morning she could stand it no longer, she had dressed and begun packing. The ornaments she had bought to decorate the room, her kitchen utensils, books, clothes, were all packed and she was ready to leave by eight.

She sat through her lectures that day in a state of weary anxiety. Where was she to go? What was she to do?

The professor had mumbled on. Occasionally he paused in his lecture on nineteenth century French literature, rested back on his heels, jutting his large stomach even further forward, and gazed round the circular amphitheatre to see how his students were reacting to his

words. A few, seated at the front of the auditorium, scribbled fervently. Others were obviously less enthralled.

The professor was afflicted with a speech impediment and was difficult to hear. Students would gradually crane forward, only to reel back, deafened, as he burst forth into a quotation from Verlaine's famous sonnet to Victor Hugo:

'Nul parmi vos flatteurs
*   d'aujourd'hui n'a connu*
Mieux que moi la fierté d'admirer
*   votre gloire:*
Votre nom m'enivrait comme un
*   nom de victoire,*
Votre oeuvre, je l'aimais d'un
*   amour ingénu.'*

'Only time I can hear him is when he starts to declaim,' a student next to Miss Frayle said. 'Then he gives me heart-failure. I'm sure he does it to make sure we stay awake.'

Miss Frayle had giggled at her. 'I can hardly understand a word. And I'm afraid my thoughts keep wandering.'

'You don't look up to much,' the other had said frankly. 'Anything wrong?'

Miss Frayle had blushed. 'I'll tell you about it afterwards,' she said to the student. She had pulled herself together and given her attention to the lecture on nineteenth century French literature. The subject was among the most fascinating of her studies, a pity the professor was so bizarre.

As his voice boomed forth, Miss Frayle's neighbour was groaning quietly. Miss Frayle had glanced at her, then somebody in the gallery moved and she looked up. The amphitheatre gallery was empty save for a sprinkling of students who sat there because they wanted to leave before the end. The doors of the lower auditorium were locked by a blue-suited porter as soon as a lecture began and opened only when it was over.

When the lecture ended, Miss Frayle had left with the other student, making their way through others of every conceivable nationality, Chinese, German, Italian, American, Swedish, Argentinian. Students came from all over

the world to enrol for the Cours de Civilisation Français, a course run by the Sorbonne to give people from foreign countries a deeper understanding of France. For herself, Miss Frayle had hardly known which to choose for her diploma studies. She had settled for French literature and L'Histoire des Idées Françaises, and whenever she could find the time she attended lectures on other subjects.

'Now then, what's your trouble?' the girl beside her said. 'You didn't hear a word of that lecture.' They had turned the arched cornerway away from the Richelieu amphitheatre and went into the cloakroom where there was a kiosk at which chocolates, cigarettes and fruit were for sale. The girl hadn't laughed when she'd told her about the umbrellas, how once again she was without a place to stay.

'My aunt has a large apartment,' the girl had said, 'and I know she'd like a bit of company. I'll take you to meet her if you like.' She had interrupted Miss Frayle's thanks. 'We've time to go and see

her before afternoon lectures, if we're quick.'

And so it had been arranged, and Miss Frayle happily occupied a room in Madame Grimault's spacious apartment.

But even now she could not view a long thin umbrella with equanimity.

Miss Frayle had searched the conglomeration of goods on the stalls of the Flea Market, she wanted to buy a very special present.

It was then that she made her first mistake. Opening her purse she took out a five-thousand franc note. A Moroccan in a red fez who had his wares on a blanket in the kerb, smiled at her. He held up various objects and called on her to admire them. Then he pointed to a sword. 'M'selle would perhaps be interested? The price is nothing, not a fraction of its real worth.'

Miss Frayle hadn't been in the least interested, but she wished to be polite, and smiled back at him. Considerably encouraged, the Moroccan held up the sword so that M'selle could see the craftsmanship, the beauty of it. It was a

genuine Samurai sword, he swore, stained with the blood of many battles. He went on to describe its astonishing history. Mesmerised by his gory tale, Miss Frayle listened, occasionally nodding.

Then, his sales-talk abruptly finishing, the man said: *'Vous êtes d'accord, M'selle.'*

There seemed no reason why she should not agree, so Miss Frayle nodded. At once the man leapt to his feet, plucked the five-thousand franc note from her hand and ceremoniously handed her the sword, hilt first. Miss Frayle gaped at the thing helplessly. *'Mais, je ne le veux pas.'*

He raised outraged hands to heaven. 'But you said you did want it,' he said firmly. 'I said, did you agree, and you nodded your head.' He gave an elaborate shrug and turned away, washing his hands of the matter. Feeling very foolish Miss Frayle could only wander miserably off. She tried vainly to hide the sword, it seemed even more cumbersome and hideous than when she had first examined it.

How on earth could she pack it, she

was thinking now as she left the Flea Market behind her. The prospect of travelling to Monte Carlo with a sword tucked under her arm was depressing. Then an even worse thought occurred to her. Whatever will Dr. Morelle say when he sees it, she wondered?

7

The manuscript in its folder lay on the desk under the window and Dyke Fenton's thoughts turned to his approaching meeting with Laking. He eyed his wrist-watch. He wasn't looking forward to it.

Laking made him uneasy these days. Dyke Fenton had sensed there had been something wrong with him for some time past. Laking had dark moods, bursts of irrational anger.

Neither Stacey nor Sara Belling seemed to have noticed anything. Or if they knew, they kept their knowledge to themselves. Stacey would surely have confided in him if she had felt there was anything off-key about her husband. Not that she was the kind of person to run to anybody for help. She was a resourceful, intelligent woman, was Stacey.

Fenton glanced at his watch again. He could make the villa in ten minutes. He'd

told Sara six o'clock when she had phoned. He presumed Laking wanted to see him about the manuscript. Or was there something else on his mind?

Fenton slipped the manuscript under his arm and let himself out of the apartment and ran lightly down the stone steps, along the terrace that skirted the building and out into the tree-lined street.

Any other time he would have enjoyed the walk. The road was shady, almost deserted. Riotously coloured flowers blazed in the gardens of the villas that skirted the road. The air was full of the scent of roses and jasmine. But Dyke Fenton's mind was already ahead of him, at the villa.

He turned into the broad road that led down the steep hillside and which passed Laking's house on its way to the road below. The slope, very steep in places, was broken up into broad wooden steps filled with gravel.

Half-way down was the pathway that led to Laking's villa. Fenton paused by the gate looking across the lawn to the terrace and the open french windows of

the library. The garden was deserted, the green-tiled, white villa silent. He pushed open the iron, decorative gates and when he got to the terrace he called a greeting.

It was Sara who answered him. She was holding some flowers and a pair of scissors. She looked cool as she came towards him, her cork-soled sandals soundless on the paving of the terrace.

'How is he?'

She looked hard at Fenton, then said non-committally: 'He looks a bit tired after the journey, but he's all right.' She raised the flowers to her face. 'Aren't they lovely?' she said. With a faint smile she turned away and went along the terrace.

Fenton saw Laking through the french windows, he was sitting at his desk, head supported on his hands, as if deep in concentration. As he went in Laking turned, 'Hello, Dyke,' he said.

Fenton went across and sat in the leather arm-chair on one side of the desk. 'Good trip?'

'Good as can be expected,' Laking said.

Fenton produced cigarettes, offered them to Laking who shook his head.

Fenton lit up and exhaled a plume of smoke on the warm air. 'I've been working on this. It's sure-fire.' He passed the manuscript across to Laking.

'What's Stacey been up to?' Laking's voice was hard.

'I guess Sara can tell you more than I can.' Fenton kept his voice level. 'I've spent all my time on the manuscript, haven't seen Stacey since you left.'

Fenton was uneasy. Laking's moods were forcing him into a world of his own. Fenton dragged at his cigarette, fixed a cheerful unconcerned look on his face. 'Everything all right in London?'

Laking's eyes were vague, his mind lost in its own strange world. 'Nothing's ever all right, Dyke,' he said quietly. 'The trip was a waste of time.' He fell into a brooding silence.

It was obvious to Fenton that Laking didn't want to tell him about the London trip. Anxious to dispel the tension, Fenton plunged into the merits of the manuscript. 'The chap's had one hell of a life,' he said. 'Shipwrecked twice, held prisoner by New Guinea head-hunters, involved in

that scandal in Italy and finally alligator-hunting up the Yangtzekiang River. Packed with good stuff, and his writing's got punch.'

Laking was still brooding. Fenton said enthusiastically: 'Won't be as big a hit as your own book was. But then you don't get two of those in a lifetime.'

Laking pushed the manuscript away as if it were a railway timetable. His face was taut, and there was a peculiar glitter in his eyes. He looked a strangely hunched, morose figure behind the desk. Dyke Fenton shifted uneasily, he found himself trying to dodge the dead stare of Laking's eyes.

Laking suddenly dropped the paper knife and leaned forward. 'I'm desperate, Fenton,' he said hoarsely. 'We've got to do something. Something drastic. I'm afraid — ' He broke off, glanced round the room, then his voice sank to a whisper. 'I'm afraid of going mad,' he said.

Fenton stared at Laking. The house was still. The rustle of trees, the evening song of a bird in the garden were a world away. Suddenly Fenton knew why he had

dreaded this visit. He had known Laking was slipping off the rails.

Dyke Fenton pulled himself together. It would be fatal to show panic. He smoothed his face into calm lines. 'You mustn't worry,' he said. 'We all get pretty close to the borderline at times.'

'Listen to me, Dyke.' Laking's voice cracked. 'It's help I need, not platitudes. You've got to back me up. There's only one way of dealing with this thing.'

'I'll do anything. You know that.'

'Then listen.' Laking ran the ivory blade of the paper-knife on the desk across the tops of his fingers, but his eyes were on Dyke Fenton. 'You know I went to London to see a doctor. He found nothing organically wrong. He said it's my mind. I could have told him. He wants me to see a psychiatrist.' He laughed harshly. 'As if that's any good.'

So this was it, Dyke Fenton thought, while he said: 'But psychiatric treatment can work wonders — '

He broke off as Laking wagged the knife at him. The blade gleamed. 'Shock treatment, insulin — ' Laking got up from

the desk, began to pace the library. He said softly: 'I know what I can take. I still know what's best for me and for Stacey. You'll have to help me with the idea I've worked out.'

Fenton watched him anxiously. What was the man driving at? Laking was still prowling. 'The bulk of my money is invested in life insurance,' he was saying. 'All the policies have the usual suicide clause. If I take my own life Stacey will lose every penny I've invested. So it'll have to be done a different way.' He stared at Dyke Fenton. 'That's where you come in.'

He felt he was struggling in some nightmare. He tried to look like an executive at a business conference, but the business was death. He prayed for Stacey or Sara to walk in and put an end to the macabre farce, but the house was silent. It might have been dead of night. He'd have to see this through alone, and whatever crazy schemes Laking's deranged mind had cooked up, he'd have to play the sympathetic friend.

'You know you can count on me, Ian,'

he said soothingly. 'We'll get things right between us.' Laking nodded like a contented child.

'That's better,' Laking said. 'I knew you'd see it my way. And it's very simple. There's no risk to you at all.'

'What do you want me to do?'

'Shoot me in the back.'

Dyke Fenton moved forward as if to say something, but Laking held up his hand. 'I've planned everything,' he said quietly. 'We'll get Sara and Stacey out of the way for an hour. No one will know you're here. We'll turn everything in the desk upside-down. Provide the motive. I'll have been murdered by a thief, person or persons unknown stuff.'

Horror drenched Fenton, holding him rigid, cleaving his tongue to the roof of his mouth. Laking went on talking, full of childish pleasure at his own ingenuity.

'You will arrive here after dark. The light on my desk will be burning. The french windows will be open wide and I shall be sitting here working with my back to you. Just as I was when you came in just now. You'll shoot from the window.

There must be no mistake. It will take only a few seconds, then you will leave, unseen, unheard, leaving no possible trace of your visit. You see how simple it is?'

Dyke Fenton knew now Laking was a raving lunatic. 'I can't do it, Ian,' he said helplessly. 'I'd be a murderer.'

Laking said quietly: 'Is it murder to put a human being out of his misery?'

'But I'd never get away with it.' He tried to enlist Laking's sympathy. 'I'd be seen leaving. The report of the gun would alert the neighbourhood. I wouldn't stand a cat in hell's chance.'

Laking had moved round the desk and opened a drawer. Fenton saw an automatic pistol in his hand. Laking laid it on the desk, on top of the manuscript.

I've got to play for time, Fenton thought. There must be something he could say that would get through the fog of Laking's insanity. He could feel the sweat sticking his shirt to his back. He stared at the automatic.

'You've got to do it, Dyke.' Laking gave a grisly smile. 'You a good shot?'

'Pretty good.' The words stuck in Dyke Fenton's throat. He was mesmerized by the pistol.

'Like the look of the gun?' Laking said. He picked it up, cradled it in his hand. It was a .45 Colt automatic, its five-inch barrel fitted with a silencer; it weighed thirty-nine ounces, and it glinted dully evil. 'You see it's fitted with a silencer. There'll be no noise. A puff of smoke, nothing more. You just squeeze the trigger.'

For a moment Laking fondled the gun affectionately. Then, gripping the barrel, he pressed the butt into Fenton's hand.

8

The feel of the gun in his hands brought Dyke Fenton a moment of enormous relief. He'd had a sudden horrible idea that Laking was going to use it there and then, on him.

He took a deep breath. He had to think fast. He hid his thoughts behind a calm mask as though seriously considering Laking's fantastic proposition as a logical way out of his dilemma. Laking had overwhelmed his last objection by revealing the silencer on the gun. Fenton pretended to study it, turning it over and examing it. The flat, heavy Colt was loaded all right. It could pump its heavy bullet into its target with man-stopping deadliness. Surreptitiously he made sure the safety catch was on.

He glanced up. Laking was watching him closely, his eyes aglow with a kind of fanatical triumph. He is insane, Fenton

thought, cold sweat breaking out on him again.

Laking said: 'Killing is the easiest thing in the world. You must remember, Dyke, you'll be performing a merciful duty.'

Fenton knew now the only thing to do was to play along with Laking. He had to convince him he was ready to co-operate, that after the first shock of dismay he had come round to thinking Laking was right. There would be time to forestall the grisly plan, time to tell Stacey of her husband's mental state, the crazy scheme he had dreamed up.

'When?' he said.

'Tonight,' Laking said.

Dyke Fenton ran his tongue over his lips. The realization that he wasn't going to have that much time to get help was like a blow bruising his already agonized nerves. But he gave a nod. His expression relaxed.

'What time tonight?' he said.

'Late, when they'll have gone to bed,' Laking said. He nodded to himself, as if this idea was newly thought up, and met his approval. 'You'll drop the gun in the

sea,' he said next. He went back to his pacing. 'I told you, Dyke, there's no risk. The plan is foolproof. I knew you'd do it for me. You understand.'

Fenton found it difficult to believe he was talking about murder. He kept reminding himself he was only playing a macabre game, even if Laking was in deadly earnest.

Laking pushed a box of cigarettes across to Fenton, who slipped the gun into his pocket, leaned forward and took a cigarette. Laking didn't smoke but he waited until Fenton had lit his own.

'I shall make some excuse to Stacey about having to work late,' he was saying. He indicated the manuscript Dyke Fenton had brought. 'I shall come in here. You will be waiting, you will see the desk-lamp go on and I'll come to the windows and open them. I shall disarrange the papers on my desk, pull out the drawers and scatter the contents. When you see me sit at the desk that'll be your cue.'

Fenton dragged at his cigarette, frowning, giving the impression he was

weighing everything carefully. 'One point,' he said at length, 'I've usually been here with you in the evenings. What about tonight?'

'You act in exactly the same way as before. When Stacey and Sara go to bed, you leave. I won't have said anything about working late, until after you've gone.'

'I see.' Fenton wanted only one thing now. To bring the nightmarish scene to a close and get out of the villa. He felt he'd played his part pretty convincingly, he felt confident, but it had been a strain. He leaned over and tapped the ash off his cigarette into an ash-tray. 'All right, Ian,' he said slowly. 'It seems I can't talk you out of it, so I might as well save my breath. If that's what you want.' The door. He would walk slowly to the door. He said, keeping his voice level, steady: 'I understand what I've got to do. If there's nothing more I'll be getting back to the apartment, now. See you tonight, as you say. I'll look in for coffee and a brandy. And after that.' He patted his pocket which held the gun.

Laking's face was moist, his eyes bright. Obviously he felt pleased with himself. He came round the desk and suddenly offered Dyke his hand. Dyke took it, surprised by Laking's abrupt change of mood. He seemed almost normal. As if now the lunatic scheme was settled he could revert to his old personality, become again the cheerful confident business associate he used to be. Before his mind went.

Why had it gone? Fenton wondered. What had unseated his reason? Insanity didn't overtake a man unless something pretty drastic happened to him. There was something here Fenton didn't understand.

'You've always backed me up, Dyke, and I knew when you understood everything you wouldn't fail me this time. Have a drink before you go.' He turned away, crossing to the cabinet. He opened it with steady hands and took out a decanter and glasses.

Another delay. Dyke Fenton clenched his nails in his palms. Why was Laking keeping him here? He must find Stacey.

There was a lot to be done. And fast. Did Laking suspect what was in his mind? Hadn't he fooled him, after all? Did he really know that he was going to raise the alarm? Tell Stacey? Laking must have realized that was the risk he was running, when he unfolded his crazy idea to him. Fenton presumed he'd felt sure he could talk him into it.

He plunged his hand in his pocket and his fingers closed over the heavy Colt. He must get rid of it. He didn't even want to take it out of the house. He'd have to hide it somewhere, a place where Laking would never find it. But where?

'Same as usual, Dyke?'

'Thanks.' Fenton took the gin and tonic from the man he was in a few hours' time supposed to shoot in the back.

Laking raised his own glass. 'Here's to success,' he said with grim humour.

Fenton gulped his drink quickly and went across to the door. Laking was watching him. He felt sure the other must realize that he hadn't talked him into it, and would stop him. With terrific relief he saw Laking sit at his desk again.

Fenton went out into the hall and now he began to tremble violently all over. As he turned to hurry out of the house he noticed the long chest that stood below the banisters. He lifted the lid and buried the revolver under the motoring rugs. He lowered the lid into place gently. He expected Laking's voice, suddenly calling him back.

But there was no sound from the man he'd left and he went swiftly out.

9

He had to see Stacey. That was the first thing he had to do. He wondered where Sara was, he could have made it sound casual and left a message with her for Stacey to phone him. Only that might be risky, he thought. Laking might hear her phoning him and put two and two together. He daren't tell Sara the truth, God knows how she would take it.

Dyke Fenton paused at the gates and looked around him as if expecting Stacey to materialize, but he was quite alone. He stood there for some moments, dragging at his cigarette while the paralysing shock of what Laking had told him slowly subsided. Then he went out of the gate, throwing a fleeting glance towards the villa. But no one was to be seen.

He let himself into his apartment, poured himself a stiff drink and stared through the window in the direction of Laking's villa. How to get hold of Stacey,

that was the problem. He began phoning round the Lakings' friends, in the hope that someone might know where she was. But he drew blank each time. She hadn't been seen since lunchtime, the people she'd lunched with, an American journalist and his wife and family, whom the Lakings knew best in Monte Carlo, said that Stacey had left to return to the Villa des Fleurs. Fenton had to make his inquiries seem casual as he asked the people if they should meet up with Stacey to tell her he'd been asking for her.

He couldn't even leave messages for her to phone him, in case she did so from her own villa, when Laking might, almost certainly would, know of it. Taut with frustration he hung up on the last phone call that he could think of to make, and stared out of the window. There was nothing he could do but wait, it would be useless to go rushing out looking for her.

With a sudden shiver he realized that Laking was a potential danger to anyone at the villa. If he was crazy enough to dream up a scheme like this he was capable of doing some harm to Stacey. Or

Sara. If either of them thwarted him, even unintentionally, that twisted mind might explode into violence.

Dyke Fenton began to sweat. What had happened to Laking? What had plunged him into this nightmare world of madness? He'd noticed the gradual change in his boss's attitude but he couldn't remember how long ago it had first become apparent.

Laking had always been moody, but the moods had grown darker in recent months. He was easily roused to anger, he had become increasingly impatient and irritable. Fenton had put these things down to some passing phase of Laking's, and had shrugged them off as best he could. Laking had always had his bad patches, but there had been the other times when he was most charming.

Fenton thought he heard footsteps outside his apartment. He rushed out into the hall and opened the door. His hopes crashed. It wasn't Stacey, only the occupant of the next apartment, a middle-aged Frenchman who spoke to him in a strong Parisian accent and then

went into his own apartment. Fenton closed his door and went back to the sitting-room. How much longer before he heard from Stacey? The waiting was hell. He wondered what Laking and Sara were doing. If Stacey was back there now? He debated phoning to see if she had returned, but decided against it, yet. It was too risky. He began to wish he'd taken Sara into his confidence. After all, she'd proved herself cool and efficient enough, and she might have noticed Laking's increasing moodiness and would have been half-prepared for the shock of the truth.

It was then that it occurred to Fenton that even if Sara hadn't been unaware of the deterioration in Laking's mind it was impossible to believe Stacey hadn't realized there was something wrong.

Stacey had never discussed her personal life with her husband to Fenton, but Laking's moods and depressions must have had a drastic effect on their relationship. Dyke Fenton searched his memory for anything during the past months that could have sparked off the

change in Laking's mind, but everything had followed its normal routine pattern.

There was only one small thing perhaps, but Fenton could see no reason to attach any importance to it. Laking's book. The one he had built the business on. The few occasions on which he had mentioned it, and this evening had been one, appeared to have a strange effect on Laking. The book touched some sensitive spot somewhere inside the man, brought a hostile shadow into his eyes.

Laking never wanted to talk about the book and so Dyke Fenton usually kept off the subject. But now he wondered. It was the only thing he could wonder about. There was nothing else. But it was hard to see how a book good enough to found a successful business on could wreak the kind of havoc which had befallen Laking.

He looked at his watch. It was just on six-thirty. Nearly an hour and a half since he'd seen Laking. And in a couple of hours he was supposed to be back there. To look in on Ian and Stacey Laking for coffee and a drink. And after that? Fenton wondered miserably how he was going to

tell Stacey, if and when she did show up. Fresh doubts assailed him. Had he acted rightly in leaving Sara alone with Laking? Perhaps he should have stayed at the villa until Stacey got back, then contrived to tell her without arousing her husband's suspicions.

When the doorbell pealed through the apartment he jumped as if an electric current had passed through his body. Then he stubbed his cigarette and hurried to the door.

It was Stacey. She stood there on the step. She was wearing a navy blue linen skirt and a white square-necked jersey, cut low, showing the hollow of her throat. Her suntanned legs were bare and her dark blue sandals were dust-streaked as if she had walked a long way.

It was with a sense of sudden shock that Dyke Fenton realized what a beautiful woman Stacey Laking was. Her hair was dark with auburn streaks that glowed to gold when the sun shone on it. Now it was windblown as if she had been running. Her mouth was full and wide, her eyes were a deep blue, set wide apart.

But now as Fenton looked at her he saw that her eyes were troubled. There was a lost look about her.

'Dyke,' she said. 'I had to see you.' Her voice was low, trembling on the edge of tears. Impulsively she put out her hands to him. Fenton took them, surprised to find how cold her touch was. So she knew already? How? Who had told her?

'Thank God you've come,' he said. They were in the sitting-room. As he turned to her she put her hands up to her face, tears streamed down her cheeks. 'Dyke, it's awful.'

He put a comforting arm round her shoulders, bewildered by her loss of control. Had Laking himself told her of his grisly scheme? He looked down at her, oddly moved by her grief, feeling a great tenderness for her.

'You got my message?'

She looked up at him from wet eyes. 'What message?'

Fenton frowned. 'I've been leaving messages all over Monte Carlo for you.' She shook her head with bewilderment. So Laking had told her. She had gone

back to the villa and he'd told her the whole mad business. 'So you've seen Ian,' he said, his voice leaden.

'No,' Stacey said. 'I haven't been to the villa since this morning.' Suddenly she began to choke with uncontrollable sobs. 'I — I couldn't face Ian.'

10

Dyke Fenton stared at Stacey in dismay. Had something else happened? Why had she rushed here to see him? Why was she so upset if she hadn't come from the villa? From Laking? Something else must be wrong, badly wrong.

Her tears roused a dormant anger in him against whoever it was had upset her. He said roughly: 'You'd better have a drink. Help you pull yourself together.'

She wiped her eyes with the back of her hand the way a child does, and watched him pour her a brandy and soda. She had stopped crying but her hand shook as she sipped the drink. She was very pale under the suntan. Dyke saw that she was pretty close to a breakdown.

'Cigarette?'

She shook her head. He lit a cigarette for himself and sat beside her. She leaned towards him, grasping his hand with cold fingers.

'Dyke,' she said. 'You're the only one I can really trust. I've never told you about my life with Ian, but — I — ' She broke off and took a drink. 'Dyke, you've got to help me, you know Ian. You must have noticed his strange behaviour. Dyke, you've got to help me to get away.'

It was a second shock, as hard to take as the first. Fenton didn't know what to say. He knew what was coming, he supposed he'd known all the time that things had in fact been amiss between Stacey and Laking. Even though they'd put a good front on it, played happily married. He knew Stacey well enough to know she must have fought against the impending disaster, but now she was beaten to a stand-still.

'It's impossible to go on.' Stacey's voice shook. 'His terrible moods and the hateful insane things he says to me.' She choked. 'I've tried — God knows, I've tried, but I can't bear to be in the same room with him. Dyke, I'm afraid of him.' She hesitated. Even now, Fenton thought she doesn't want to rat on him. 'I've had to lock my bedroom door. And these last

few months he's been unbearable. It's just a hell.'

Fenton abruptly got up, went to fetch himself a drink. 'What's made him like this? What devil drove him?'

'I don't know,' she said helplessly. 'I've done nothing to provoke him, but wherever I go, whatever I suggest, there's always something wrong.'

'You know he went to London to see a doctor?' She was staring at him blankly. 'He's been recommended to a psychiatrist for treatment. But he says he doesn't believe in them.'

'I — I didn't know. Poor Ian.' She turned away. 'But even if he gets better,' she said without looking at Fenton, 'it wouldn't help me. It's too late. I can't go back to him. Ever again.' She faced him again. Her tear-stained face made him move towards her impulsively. 'I've been wandering around ever since lunch. I felt so ill with thinking about my life, horrible sickening thoughts. I've been trying to decide what to do.' Her voice steadied. 'I made up my mind. I'm never going back. And then I found myself here at your

apartment. I know you'll help me. And you will, Dyke, you will?'

Suddenly she was in his arms. He felt her body trembling. 'Of course,' he said gently. 'I'll do anything I can. You know that.'

The closeness of her body, her scent she invariably used, and the soft vibrance of her hair under his hand made his blood race. Warning lights flashed in his brain. He would have to fight against his own feelings. With her in his arms he realized that their friendship, until now entirely innocent, held the seeds of something much deeper.

Tragedy had blasted away the barriers, revealing deeper emotions. But they must be smothered, now, at once, before one or the other put them into words.

Laking was insane, she had run to Dyke for comfort, but she was still Laking's wife, and this was no time to forget that. Not only because of Laking's crazy scheme, but also because it was his mental illness which had estranged her from him.

Fenton gently eased Stacey into a chair.

He picked up her half-emptied glass and put it in her hand.

'Knock it back,' he said. 'You must pull yourself together.'

Stacey did as he told her. Her eyes were dry now. She sat watching him with all the trust of a child.

'I've been waiting for you to get in touch with me,' he said. 'I wanted you to know how bad a state Ian is in. I didn't know how much you've gone through already. All the same this will come as a shock.' His eyes searched her face.

'Tell me,' she said quietly. 'Nothing can shock me now. I've been living in dread too long. Tell me what it is.'

Still Fenton hesitated. Then he said slowly: 'He wants to die.' He told her about his meeting with her husband. 'He wants everything to come to you, but because of his heavy investments in insurance policies he can't commit suicide. He tried to get me to promise to kill him. To shoot him.'

Her sudden intake of breath was loud in the quiet room. She clutched at her throat as the terrifying implication dawned

on her. 'My God,' she said. 'What a horrible thing. To — to implicate you.' She shook her head as if to shake away the evil thought. 'If only I'd realized all this,' she said, 'This alters everything.'

'He's got it all worked out,' Fenton said wearily. 'It would look like some burglar. Person or persons unknown. He was in such a bad way I thought he might do something violent there and then. He produced a gun, the one he wants me to use. He acted and talked like a madman.'

'And so?'

'I pacified him by playing along with him. I pretended to agree. I promised to shoot him.' He told her everything that had transpired.

'Where's the gun, Dyke?'

'I hid it in the chest in the hall,' he said.

Stacey got up suddenly. She was trembling and white-faced. 'I must go back,' she said, making an effort to keep her voice calm. 'Sara is alone with him.'

Fenton sensed her fear and he said steadily: 'I'm sure there's nothing to be afraid of at this moment. So long as he thinks I'm going to play my part he'll be

content. And he thinks I've got the gun. He's got to be looked after. He needs treatment without delay.'

Stacey turned to him. Her fingers tightened on his arm. 'He'll wonder where I am. He might get suspicious.' She bit into her lower lip. 'I must talk to him.'

Fenton hesitated. 'You're not going back there alone, Stacey. Not after all you've been through. I'm coming with you.'

She nodded dazedly. 'We can't do anything until I've talked to him,' she said. 'Then we must decide what's best. There must be help we can get.' Her voice trailed hopelessly.

She let Fenton take her arm as they went out of the apartment. They walked quickly, silently to the Villa des Fleurs. It was dusk now. The lights of Monte Carlo below glittered like jewels against the shadowy background of the sea. Early stars flickered in the pale sky, the air was warm and the shadows of the trees wrapped themselves softly around Fenton and the woman beside him.

They reached the iron gate and paused.

The silent air of the garden was heavy with the scent of flowers. A light glowed against the ghostly whiteness of the villa and Dyke Fenton could see that the french windows opening on to the terrace stood open as they had been when he'd gone in to find Laking earlier. But no sound came from within.

Fenton pushed open the gate and led the way to the terrace. He turned to Stacey. 'Ian must be there,' he said. He found himself speaking in a low voice. 'Sure you want to go in?'

She nodded. 'You'd better let me go first. Wait outside and come in after a few minutes as if we'd arrived separately. If he sees us together he'll know you've told me everything.'

Dyke Fenton hated to let her go but what she said made sense. Laking mustn't think Stacey knew anything, not yet anyway.

He kept in the shadows while Stacey went to the french windows. She stood there and she moved no further. She gave a sudden choking gasp that started to build into a scream and then Fenton

came running. He stared into the room, then went towards the desk.

Ian Laking lay sprawled forward in his chair, his head lying across the desk in a grotesque attitude. Fenton moved towards him. Then he stopped.

Laking had been shot in the back.

11

Stacey came slowly towards the crumpled figure at the desk, walking with the stiff jerky steps of some puppet-doll. Her eyes were staring with shock, her face deathly pale. She paused on the far side of the desk watching Fenton as he moved round the body.

All Dyke Fenton could think of was that Laking had died in just the same way as he had planned. Only someone else had killed him. He had been shot from the french windows as he sat at the desk and the motive looked like robbery. The desk-drawers were thrown open and their contents scattered on the floor. Everything had worked out the way Laking's crazed brain had wanted it, except that it had happened a few hours earlier.

And Dyke Fenton hadn't done it.

Who had? Someone else, who knew what Laking had planned. But who could have known? Who else could Laking have

told? Who else would he have told when the whole object of his plan was that it should remain secret, the business of the life-insurance necessitated that.

Fenton saw the two glasses at one corner of the desk. The glasses he and Laking had drunk from. He glanced at the body again. Laking's face was hidden in the crook of his arm. He wondered what that crazed fool was thinking now, wherever he was. Was he laughing ironically at the way the bad joke he'd made had gone sour on him?

Fenton moved to Stacey's side. 'Just the way he planned it,' he said, and hardly recognized the croaking whisper as his own voice.

She shivered, turned away hiding her face in her hands. 'Who could have done it?'

'The police will find that out.' He took her arm. 'You'd better get out of the room. I'll close the windows.'

She stopped at the door. 'Do it now, Dyke. I'll wait for you.'

He went back across the room, closed and locked the french windows and then

impulsively he pulled the long curtains together, as if to shut out the sight from the inquisitive night. They both went into the hall and closed the door behind them.

'Better tell Sara,' Fenton said.

'Surely she must have heard?' Stacey said, bewildered.

Fenton recalled the silencer on the Colt automatic. Stacey called Sara as Fenton crossed to the chest. He lifted the lid. The gun was gone. Incredulously he pulled the rugs out on to the floor. But the gun was not there.

Stacey turned to stare at Dyke as he jumbled the rugs back into the box and closed the lid.

'The gun,' he said to her. 'It's gone.'

'Are you sure?' There was a high frightened note in her voice.

'I told you I slipped it in here out of the way so Ian shouldn't find it. Now it isn't here.'

She said frowning: 'Who would know you put it there?'

He passed his hand across his forehead wearily. 'I just can't fathom it, unless Ian saw me hide it, but I left him at his desk.

I'm sure I was careful about that.'

'The police will have to sort it out, Dyke,' she said. 'But where's Sara?' She called out again, but there was no answer.

'That's odd,' Fenton said. 'She must be out. She didn't tell me she was going anywhere when I saw her.'

Stacey gripped his arm. 'Dyke, you don't think something's happened to her?'

He felt the colour drain from his face. 'Of course not,' he said with forced confidence. 'But we'd better make sure she's not here.' He quickly looked into the other downstairs rooms but there was no sign of Sara. Anxious now, they hurried upstairs together and along to her room. That was empty too.

Stacey was clutching Fenton's arm as though drawing strength from it. She began talking fast, as if it gave her comfort. She told him how that more than ever before she needed his friendship. She knew she ought to rely on her own strength, Dyke had enough to worry about. There was one crumb of comfort in the whole tragic business. Ian's death

was a terrible shock but it had brought her release from an impossible situation. She must cling to that knowledge at this ghastly time. Above all she must not panic. She wished Sara would return. 'I wonder how long she's been gone,' Stacey said.

'I should have warned her,' Dyke Fenton said. 'I should have told her the state Ian was in. Then she wouldn't have gone out and left him.'

Sara clutched his arm tightly. 'You mustn't talk like that,' she said fiercely. 'You're not to blame. Ian may have sent her out. She couldn't have refused, even if you'd warned her not to leave him.'

They went down the wide staircase, while an eerie silence seemed to wrap itself around the villa and the atmosphere lay heavy and sombre.

'I'll ring the police,' Fenton said. Then a doctor, he thought. Not that he could be of any use. Laking was past that kind of help. As he picked up the telephone receiver that stood by the chest in the hall, the shrill pealing of the doorbell

flooded the Villa des Fleurs. They both jumped.

'Must be Sara,' Stacey said, and she went and opened the front door. 'Forgotten her key,' she said and then wondered why in that case the front-door had been locked.

Fenton paused from speaking into the telephone as he saw a tall, gaunt figure silhouetted against the dusk of the twilight, and heard a voice say: 'I am Dr. Morelle. I have called to see Mr. Laking.'

'Oh, yes, of course.' Stacey was flustered. Fenton put the telephone receiver down. 'I'm Mrs. Laking,' Stacey said.

Dyke Fenton came forward involuntarily. He had read newspaper stories featuring Dr. Morelle's criminological activities. And he was a psychiatrist of world-wide fame, Fenton knew.

Looking at Dr. Morelle now, Fenton could only feel a sudden chill. The strong, gaunt face, the hooded eyes, the enigmatic expression, were not suggestive of sympathy. But what was he doing here,

turning up out of the blue? He stood beside Stacey.

'Afraid you're too late to see Mr. Laking, Dr. Morelle,' Dyke Fenton said slowly. 'He's dead.'

12

Stacey Laking stood looking at Dr. Morelle as if he had mesmerized her with those hooded eyes. She too knew of his fame as a psychiatrist and criminologist, but what was he doing in Monte Carlo? Then she seemed to recall some mention someone had made to her about the great Dr. Morelle having moved into the Villa Midnight, while the Comtesse who owned it was away in America. But what was he doing here, at this time of all times?

They were in the hall now, and Dr. Morelle's expression provided no answer to her spinning thoughts, nor did it give any indication of his reaction to what Dyke Fenton had told him. Dr. Morelle spoke quietly to her, and Stacey was not sure if there was a glimmer of sympathy in his dark eyes.

'I am sorry, Mrs. Laking. What has happened?'

'He's been murdered,' Dyke Fenton said flatly. 'Shot in the back. Just now.'

Dr. Morelle's only sign of interest was the almost imperceptible lift of an eyebrow. 'Where is he?'

'In there,' Fenton said with a movement of his head. 'We found him when we came in a few minutes ago.'

Dr. Morelle turned to Stacey. He suggested she should wait while they went into the other room. No point in inflicting any further distress on herself. She nodded gratefully and Fenton led Dr. Morelle into the library.

Fenton stood near the door, watching the tall sombre figure as he made a brief examination. Dr. Morelle did not disturb the body or remove anything on the desk but Dyke Fenton was sure those dark hooded eyes missed nothing.

Dr. Morelle crossed to the curtains, drew them aside and opened the french windows. He stood and faced the body, obviously making some calculation. Then he came back into the room, closed the windows and pulled the curtains together again. All his actions were methodical, as

if each was important in itself.

'The french windows were open,' Fenton said, 'and the curtains drawn back when we came in by way of the garden.'

Dr. Morelle's eyes raked over Laking and the untidy desk again. 'This would suggest the motive was robbery,' he said. 'But that may be merely to offer a false impression. There seems little doubt the killer acted more in the crisis of some emotion than for any cold-blooded reason of material gain.' He picked up a book which was partially covered by the manuscript which Fenton had left on the desk. He seemed to be suddenly interested in it, then he replaced it exactly where it had lain before. His eyes moved over the body again. 'Where the shots are placed, any one was fatal. He would certainly have been dead when the first was fired. Yet three shots were fired in all. Why fire three times, when once was sufficient?' He regarded Fenton levelly.

Dyke Fenton could only nod dumbly. Dr. Morelle would have to be told everything, but where and how to begin? He reflected that by reason of his

profession Dr. Morelle would at least believe the story, however fantastic it sounded. Who better than he to understand the tortuous stresses of the human mind?

'Had Laking any enemies?' Dr. Morelle's question cut across Fenton's halting explanation of what had transpired earlier.

'Not as far as I know,' Fenton said truthfully. 'He was well enough liked, although lately his illness had made him pretty trying to those who lived and worked close to him.'

'Towards Mrs. Laking, and yourself, in fact?'

'Mrs. Laking had suffered a lot, though she's concealed it from everyone.' Fenton felt Dr. Morelle watching him keenly. There was no point in trying to hide anything from him. 'And I was finding him difficult to get on with, but I put it down to a passing mental phase. I didn't realize how serious his condition was.'

'How long have you been here this evening?'

'Mrs. Laking and I came back together only a few minutes ago. We can't have

been here more than ten minutes.'

'You have telephoned for the police?'

'I was just going to when you arrived.'

Dr. Morelle merely nodded. 'There is something I ought to discuss with you and Mrs. Laking before the police come,' he said.

Fenton had a sudden chilling feeling Dr. Morelle knew more about Laking's death than he had so far revealed. But how on earth could he? No one knew about it, except himself and Stacey. Dr. Morelle's expression was enigmatic, it told Fenton nothing. What did he want to discuss with Stacey and himself?

'When did you last see Laking alive?'

'At about a quarter to six this evening. He'd just got back from London and he asked me to come over. I wanted to see him anyway, to discuss a new book.'

Fenton indicated the manuscript in its folder which still lay on one corner of the desk.

Dr. Morelle glanced at it, then back to Fenton. 'What about Mrs. Laking? When did she last see her husband?'

'She hadn't seen him since he went to

London,' Fenton said slowly. 'She went out to lunch with some friends this morning. Then a little while ago she called at my apartment and we came on here together, and,' his eyes strayed involuntarily towards the desk, 'and found him.'

Dr. Morelle glanced once more round the room and then moved towards the door. 'I think we should rejoin Mrs. Laking now. You would probably like me to explain the reason for my unexpected arrival.'

Fenton gave a wry smile. 'I've been puzzling why you came, but I'm certainly glad you're here. Murder is something out of my line. But you're an expert.'

As he said it he realized it wasn't the most suitable remark to have made, it was his nervousness which had allowed him to drop the brick, but as he glanced at Dr. Morelle he decided there was no telling whether he had taken it as a compliment or otherwise. Dyke Fenton gained the notion that neither tributes nor denigration would make any impression on him. Nothing would sway him from his set

purpose. He followed Dr. Morelle out into the hall. Then he led the way past the two nude statues to the next room, where Stacey was awaiting them.

Her face was drawn into a frown and her eyes were dull. Even so, Fenton realized, looking across at her, there was a beauty in her face that nothing would ever eradicate. She stood by a low table and looked at the gaunt figure of Dr. Morelle.

'Can I get you anything?' she asked. 'A drink, a cigarette?'

Dr. Morelle shook his head. 'I was just explaining to Mr. Fenton that there is something I wish to explain to you both. I would rather we had no distractions at all while you listen.'

He glanced at Fenton who stood with his hands in his jacket pockets. Stacey sat on the edge of an arm-chair, Dyke Fenton stood behind her, his hands pushed with a kind of desperate dejection deep into his pockets. In the soft glow of the lamp-light from the ornate electric-lamps, Dr. Morelle seemed to tower above them.

'I am staying in Monte Carlo,' Dr.

Morelle said. 'At the Villa Midnight.' A grim smile flicked across his face and quickly vanished. 'My idea was to get away from London and Harley Street so that I could work quietly and undisturbed on a matter of some importance to me. I hardly anticipated that anyone locally would be getting in touch with me.'

Stacey frowned at him. Did this tie up with Laking's visit to the doctor in London? He had said something about having been advised to see a psychiatrist. And here was Dr. Morelle on the doorstep. 'Laking? But he only returned from London to-day.'

Dr. Morelle took from his inside pocket an envelope. 'He must have written it as soon as he arrived, and posted it at once.' He extracted the folded sheet from the envelope. 'It bears this afternoon's post-mark.'

'Pretty quick all the same,' Fenton said.

'One of those twists of fortune,' Dr. Morelle said dryly. 'The postman who collected it from the postbox happened to notice this particular letter, and since he also chanced to be passing the villa this

evening, he thought he would save time and drop it in. A trifle out of normal routine, but after all the people of the South are inclined to believe that Man came before rules and regulations.' He unfolded the letter and looked impassively at them over it. 'It's message was such that I came straight along here.' Dr. Morelle's expression had grown grim.

'What did he say?' Stacey's voice was hoarse.

'I will read it,' Dr. Morelle said. 'I beg you not to interrupt until I have finished.'

Fenton suddenly clenched his hands. Stacey looked quickly across at him. It must be pretty urgent, Fenton thought, or why should Dr. Morelle have come round so soon after reading it. Stacey could see through the paper that it was written in ink in her husband's handwriting, but that was all. She caught Dr. Morelle's eye and then he began to read.

'Dear Dr. Morelle,' he read aloud. 'Sir Trevor Kirkland will be writing to you about my case but I fear he may be too late. For some time now I have been suffering acute mental distress, the direct

cause of which is the clandestine relationship which exists between my wife and my righthand man in my publishing business, Dyke Fenton.'

Dr. Morelle broke off as both Stacey and Fenton started to speak. 'You must let me finish,' he said.

'I did not tell Sir Trevor,' Dr. Morelle continued reading, as Dyke Fenton and Stacey stared incredulously first at him then at each other and then back to Dr. Morelle once more, 'of this situation. I could not force myself to do it. I should have been reluctant to tell you, but that matters have now reached a point where my life is in danger and I ask urgently for your help. Fenton plans to kill me so that he can get my wife. I suspect he is arranging to do it tonight. I beg you to get here as soon as possible. I can give you proof that all this is true. Please, I need your help. I need it urgently. Ian Laking.'

'The rotten, insane swine,' Fenton said violently. 'It's mad, vicious nonsense.'

'He would do anything,' Stacey said, in a low harsh voice. 'Say anything.'

Dr. Morelle folded the letter and returned it to his pocket, and as he watched him do so Fenton thought with a dull sort of frustrated bitterness: he's afraid I'll try and get it from him.

Stacey looked up at Dr. Morelle. She was white-faced and trembling all over. 'You don't believe it, do you?' she said, framing the words with difficulty.

'Of course he doesn't,' Fenton broke in roughly. 'Dr. Morelle knows as well as we do that Laking was out of his mind. A vicious, revengeful, crazy monster.'

Dr. Morelle looked first at Fenton, then at Stacey. 'All I know is that he is dead,' he said.

13

Dyke Fenton took out cigarettes and lit one with trembling fingers. He was trying to collect his thoughts, to understand the terrifying situation Laking had involved him in. Laking had framed him, that was the stark, hideous truth. But why, why?

There had never been anything between himself and Stacey. Nothing in their behaviour could ever have given Laking grounds for one minute's jealousy. This evening in his apartment had been the first time he had thought of her as anything other than Laking's wife. When her confession of disillusion and misery had awoken a dormant response in him.

Yet it was obvious that for a long time Laking must have secretly nursed an insane jealousy. And now he was dead, murdered, and he had left behind him a damning letter. How could Dyke disprove what Laking said? Who was there to prove the dead man's insanity?

Fenton brushed a shaking hand across his face. The police had to be called in, and with the letter in their hands things looked black. He had to get Dr. Morelle on his side, had to persuade him to hold on to the letter. He had to convince Dr. Morelle of the truth if he was to escape from the cunning deadly trap Laking had sprung on him.

How had Laking worked things out? Dr. Morelle shouldn't have received the letter until next morning. It was only by the merest million-to-one accident that it had been delivered this evening. He couldn't possibly have foreseen that. He must have reckoned on Fenton only pretending to co-operate in his grisly plan. Laking must have calculated that he would divulge the whole thing to Stacey, as in fact he had done. And he had worked out some bright idea, all unknown to Fenton, of bringing Dr. Morelle on the scene next night, just in time to catch Fenton in some act which would make him appear to be about to murder Laking.

Fenton shuddered. He'd been fooled utterly into thinking that Laking meant to

end his own life. It was Fenton's life he wanted to put an end to, not his own. And then someone even more ruthless, more opportunist than Laking, had forestalled the plan, but fixing it so that the trap would still spring upon Dyke Fenton. Except that now it would appear that he actually had done the murder and not merely attempted it. As if that wasn't a tough enough spot to be in.

Dyke Fenton fingered his collar, it felt tight round his moist neck. He was perspiring, he could feel the sweat running down his temples. He had to drag out a handkerchief and dab his face. He saw Dr. Morelle extract a Le Sphinx from his case and light it. 'You realize I must telephone the police, now,' he said. 'Is there anything you wish to tell me before I do so?'

His dark, hooded glance rested on Fenton momentarily and then shifted to Stacey Laking.

'Only that we are absolutely innocent,' she said. She had got to her feet and faced Dr. Morelle. 'Of course we have always been good friends,' she threw a

glance at Fenton. 'Mr. Fenton and my husband worked together, closely. But we've never given my husband any grounds for his horrible accusations.'

She took a deep breath and looked squarely at Dr. Morelle. 'I admit my marriage has been unhappy for some time,' she said haltingly, 'because of Ian's changing attitude to me, but no one was aware of it. I may as well tell you I'd made up my mind to leave my husband. That's why I went to Mr. Fenton's apartment this evening, but then he told me about Ian and the dreadful plan he had in his mind. When he'd told me that we came straight back to the villa. We found him dead. You know that.'

Stacey shivered and put her hands to her face. With an effort she looked up again to meet the penetrating eyes of Dr. Morelle, who had said nothing, only stood there listening to her intently. 'When you have heard what he told Mr. Fenton,' she said spiritedly, 'you will have no doubts at all that Ian was insane.'

Dr. Morelle took his eyes off her and studied the cigarette-smoke ascending to

the ornate ceiling. Neither his manner nor expression gave them a hint of his reaction to what she had said. He looked across at Fenton. 'What was it he told you,' he said slowly, 'why should it suggest insanity?'

'He asked me to shoot him. To shoot him in the back.' Dyke Fenton spoke flatly.

Dr. Morelle raised a dark eyebrow. 'And when were you supposed to carry out this remarkable action?'

'Tonight. After Stacey and his secretary had gone to bed.'

'His secretary.'

'Sara Belling,' Stacey said. 'She lives here with us. She's out at the moment, but she should be back very soon.'

Dr. Morelle nodded and turned to Dyke Fenton.

'His idea was to pretend to be working on the manuscript I'd brought over,' Fenton said. 'I would have gone back to my apartment in the normal way. I was to look in here after dinner as I often did, for a drink. Then I was to slip back and steal on to the terrace. Laking would have left

the french windows open, the curtains drawn back, a light on the desk, and he would be sitting with his back to the garden, after first making things untidy to give the impression he'd been shot by a burglar.' He paused and took a deep breath. 'Then I was supposed to shoot him in the back.'

'You possess a firearm?'

'No. Laking gave it to me. He'd thought of everything. Even a silencer.'

'Where is it?'

'I don't know. It's gone from the place where I hid it. I hid it, or thought I had, in the chest in the hall as I was leaving.'

'How long ago was this?'

Fenton thought for a moment. 'It would be about six-thirty or seven. I didn't notice the time, I was in quite a flap, as you can imagine.'

Dr. Morelle stubbed his cigarette out into the ash-tray.

'Was anyone else in the house besides you and Laking?'

'Sara was here. At least I suppose she was. I'd met her when I arrived to see Laking. But I didn't see her before I left. I

did think of trying to find her to ask her to give a message to Mrs. Laking.'

'What kind of message?'

'To ask her to get in touch with me as soon as she came in. I wanted to let her know about her husband. Then I decided not to, I was afraid that the shock might be too much for her. And then, too, Laking might have overheard her talking to Mrs. Laking, and suspect that I'd given the show away. What he'd told me was deadly secret.'

'I can imagine,' Dr. Morelle said. 'You had no hint of Laking's proposition when you called here this evening?'

'Good God, no. I realized he was getting a bit difficult, moody at times, but I never suspected that he was going out of his mind. That he was so crazy jealous.' He paused. 'I'll tell you exactly how he talked,' he said, 'from the beginning.'

Dr. Morelle heard him through, his only movement was to light another Le Sphinx, now and again, giving his attention through the cigarette-smoke to Stacey Laking, who stood there, still and taut in the ornately furnished room, the

126

warm starlit night gathering round the villa outside. A flicker of interest showed in his face at the mention of Sir Trevor Kirkland's name, whom, Fenton said, the dead man had gone to London to consult.

'What else could I do but humour him,' Fenton said finally, 'pretend to fall in with his plan? I had to get time to think, to know what was best to do to help him.'

'And when you came back he was dead,' Dr. Morelle said quietly. 'Having met his death in a manner peculiarly similar to that which you had agreed to mete out to him. In accordance with his express wish, of course.'

He made a tall, brooding figure which dominated the room. 'I'll telephone the police now.'

'You can't do that,' Stacey said. 'He didn't do it.' She stepped forward as if to stop Dr. Morelle from going to the telephone. 'Dyke told you, he listened to my husband because he had to. He agreed to fall in with his idea to humour him.'

Fenton had put a hand on her arm. 'It's

all right,' he said to her. 'He's got to tell the police. Let him get it over with.'

Dr. Morelle was already at the door.

'Dr. Morelle,' Dyke Fenton said hesitantly, Dr. Morelle turned to him. 'The letter,' the other said, in a cracked voice. 'Won't they want to know about the letter he wrote you?'

'It would be impossible for me to withhold such important evidence,' Dr. Morelle said through a puff of cigarette-smoke. Then he turned on his heel and Fenton and Stacey Laking followed him quickly into the hall.

'But, Dr. Morelle,' Stacey broke off as at that moment footsteps sounded outside the front door.

Dr. Morelle stood by the hall table, his hand close to the telephone, but he did not pick up the receiver. Fenton stood beside Stacey Laking and all three of them had their eyes fixed on the door.

14

It was Sara Belling who came in, and stopped, obviously taken aback at Dr. Morelle. Her glance flickered over him, then on to Fenton, then it fastened on Stacey Laking. 'There you are,' she said. 'I thought I'd go out to meet you as an excuse for a walk. It's such a lovely evening. The stars, they look as if you can pull them out of the sky — ' She broke off with a little smile. 'I hurried back,' she said, 'when I realized I must have missed you.' She was breathing fast, unevenly.

'This is Dr. Morelle,' Fenton said. 'Miss Sara Belling.'

As she murmured appropriately to the still, remote figure by the telephone she was frowning slightly. 'I'm sure I've heard of you,' she said brightly. 'Should I have done?' Her manner jarred a little in the tense atmosphere.

'It is possible,' Dr. Morelle said.

'Dr. Morelle came to see Ian,' Stacey said quickly.

'Ian?' At once Sara Belling's expression changed. Her eyes widened with apprehension. She moved forward. 'What's happened? Is he all right?' Her gaze started towards the library. 'He was in there when I went out. I looked in to say I thought I might look out for you.' She turned back to Stacey.

Stacey gave a muffled gasp. Sara looked at her sharply. Fenton threw a quick look at Dr. Morelle whose eyes, dark and shadowed beneath the heavy brows, seemed bent upon Sara. 'He's dead, Sara,' he said.

Sara's hands flew to her face and she began to breathe in quick gulping breaths. As if, Stacey thought, she was going to cry. Colour drained from her cheeks, leaving her skin a bluish-white.

'No, he can't be. When — how?' Her voice broke. Her expression was incredulous and filled with anguish.

'He was shot,' Fenton said thickly. 'Between the time you went out and the time Stacey and I got here.'

'Shot?' the other said. 'You mean he — ?'

'No,' Stacey said. 'No, Sara, he didn't shoot himself.'

'Someone else did it for him,' Dyke Fenton said.

Sara Belling stood as if turned to stone, except for the curious cracked breathing which made her mouth quiver. She twisted round to Dr. Morelle.

'I'm afraid,' Dr. Morelle said quietly, 'that is what would appear to be the case.' He picked up the telephone and Fenton touched Stacey's arm and followed the two women into the sitting-room.

'Where is he?' Sara said, her eyes dull with shock.

'In the library,' Fenton said. 'He was shot in the back, from the french windows.'

Sara whispered something inarticulately as she slumped into a chair and buried her face in her hands. Dr. Morelle's quiet, level tones sounded from the hall as he got through to the local police-office. After a moment Sara looked up and glanced shame-facedly at Stacey.

'I'm sorry,' she said quietly. 'I'm not being much help to you, Stacey, am I? It's far worse for you.'

Stacey shrugged wearily, drained now of emotion. She turned her head towards the door, listening to Dr. Morelle's voice. 'If you ask me,' she said, 'Dyke has more to worry about than anybody.'

'I don't understand,' Sara said. 'Why Dyke?'

'Because Ian put a pretty neat noose round my neck,' Fenton said savagely. 'You tell her, Stacey.'

Sara turned a puzzled, frightened face to Stacey. She shook her head as if what she was hearing conveyed no meaning to her.

'Sara,' Stacey said calmly to her, 'you must have noticed there was something wrong with Ian, that his mind wasn't working the way it used to work.'

'Oh, no.' Sara's response was immediate, loyal. 'I know he was moody, difficult, but — '

'He was mad, Sara.' Fenton cut across her protests. 'He told me this evening he wanted me to kill him, shoot him in the

back. I had to pretend to play along, I had to humour him. After I left here he wrote to Dr. Morelle and told him I was plotting to murder him.' He gave a harsh unamused laugh. 'By an odd coincidence that's how he was killed tonight — shot in the back.'

'My God,' Sara said. 'But why did he write to him, to Dr. Morelle?'

Her question took Fenton by surprise. He looked at Stacey, as if she might know the answer, but her expression made it clear that it was as much a mystery to her. It hadn't occurred to Fenton before, his mind had been so crammed with other questions, equally baffling. But now he asked himself why had Laking picked on Dr. Morelle? He gave Sara a shrug. 'Search me,' he said.

'Perhaps Dr. Morelle can tell us,' Stacey said. Sara said, 'But I still don't understand what went on. What was Ian's idea?'

Briefly, Fenton told her what had transpired, omitting none of the salient facts. As he finished, Dr. Morelle came into the room.

'The police,' he said, 'are on their way.'

'Dr. Morelle,' Stacey said, 'something's just occurred to us. Why should my husband have written that letter to you?'

Dr. Morelle considered her for a moment. 'Obviously,' he said, 'Kirkland had advised him to get in touch with me with regard to treatment. He knew I was in Monte Carlo. I mentioned that fact to Kirkland myself when I last saw him, which was only three days ago, before I myself left London.'

'What an extraordinary coincidence,' Fenton said, 'that you should have been with Sir Trevor Kirkland only three days before he saw Laking.'

Dr. Morelle regarded him enigmatically. 'Were it not for coincidence,' he said, 'fate would play a far less important role in the scheme of things.' He turned to Sara. 'Did Mr. Laking appear quite normal when you last saw him?'

'He seemed all right to me,' she said, thinking back. 'I can't remember anything that might have given me cause to expect this. If I had, I wouldn't have gone out.'

Dr. Morelle gave her a sympathetic

murmur. She shivered and said: 'I just can't believe it could have happened in the little while I was away.' Her voice died away and then she looked at Dr. Morelle sharply. 'Mr. Fenton has just told me about the letter Mr. Laking sent you. You don't believe such a terrible thing, do you? He must have been insane — some sudden brainstorm, or something, to have written that.'

'Yes, Dr. Morelle,' Stacey said desperately. 'Surely you needn't hand it over? You must know Dyke isn't capable of anything so horrible? But once the police get hold of that letter — '

'Even if you aren't yet convinced that Mr. Laking was insane,' Sara said, 'you can't refuse Dyke time in which to defend himself.'

'Regrettably, I fear, I cannot withhold such important evidence.' Dr. Morelle's tone was uncompromising. 'Not even for a few hours.'

'Haven't you forgotten something?' Fenton said suddenly, his face grim. 'Laking wrote that letter and posted it this afternoon. In the normal way you

wouldn't have received it until tomorrow. That was when you were meant to get it. It was only by chance you got it this evening. Don't you see?'

'Yes,' Stacey said, her voice rising in excitement, 'that's true. By keeping it back until tomorrow you wouldn't be putting yourself in the wrong at all. No one would expect you to have received it until then. Surely you could wait? Just those few hours?'

Dr. Morelle stared at her, his lean, chiselled face expressionless. At that moment the doorbell rang insistently. 'That'll be the police,' Dyke Fenton said. He glanced at the others with a bitter smile. 'Shall I let them in?' he said, and went out into the hall.

A middle-aged, plump man of medium height and a dark chin followed Dyke Fenton into the sitting-room, to be introduced as Inspector Levaque. Accompanying the police-officer was a gendarme, a doctor and a photographer. They remained in the background, while Levaque talked to Dr. Morelle, having first expressed his delight at making the acquaintance of the great

criminologist from Harley Street. Then, led by Dr. Morelle, Levaque, followed by his party went into the library. Fenton, Stacey and Sara were asked to wait where they were. Fenton, going to the hall, found the gendarme outside the library-door obviously keeping an eye on the trio left behind in the sitting-room.

He said nothing to the others, but already the villa seemed to him to be filling with a cloud of suspicion. He heard the police-doctor telephoning, and then Levaque and Dr. Morelle returned, the gendarme taking up a position at the door, his square face heavy with watchfulness.

'It is most opportune,' the French detective was saying, 'that you should have called here this evening.'

There was a pause, and three pairs of eyes fastened on Dr. Morelle. Involuntarily Fenton took a step forward. This was it, he told himself grimly, and barely heard Dr. Morelle's casual reply.

'I am staying at the Villa Midnight for a few weeks.'

'Quite so, quite so,' Levaque said. 'Are

you holidaying in Monte Carlo, or is your stay a professional one?'

'A little of both,' Dr. Morelle said non-committally.

'A pity that you should have become involved in this unfortunate affair,' Levaque said. 'At the same time we should be grateful for any help you can give us.'

The invitation in the detective's tone was unmistakable. Obviously Levaque felt that Dr. Morelle could contribute a not inconsiderable amount of information relevant to the situation. Fenton, watching Dr. Morelle, saw him slip his hand into the pocket where he had put Laking's letter. Instead of the letter, however, it was his cigarette case that Dr. Morelle produced. Fenton threw a look at Stacey and Sara. He saw that Levaque's sharp little eyes were studying Stacey, who was watching Dr. Morelle.

Dr. Morelle lit a cigarette. Fenton waited, but there was no sign of the damning letter.

15

Dr. Morelle's expression told Dyke Fenton nothing, but the latter felt sure now that the eminent psychiatrist had changed his mind about handing over the letter, at least for the time being. He was going to give him a chance. The thought filled Fenton with new hope.

Only one thing. Dr. Morelle would expect him to keep nothing back if Levaque started asking him questions. Crazy though the truth might sound, he'd have to tell just that.

He realized that the Frenchman had already begun to ask Stacey a few questions. Quietly, casually almost, as if he wasn't really interested in the answers. But Fenton saw Dr. Morelle's eyes fixed intently on Levaque.

'You have said that you spent most of the day away from the villa. And then you call on Monsieur Fenton, though you know your husband must have returned

from London. But you do not come back here. You call instead on Monsieur Fenton, and as a result of what he tells you about your husband, you both return here, and find he has been murdered? That is so?' Levaque's English was quite fluent.

'That's right,' Stacey said.

'Why do you not come here to see your husband on his safe return?'

'Because I was making up my mind to leave him,' Stacey said in a low voice. 'I knew there'd be a scene. And all these months I'd kept my unhappiness to myself. But I couldn't do it any longer. I had to talk to someone. And so I went to see Mr. Fenton. He's been a friend of my husband for some time and I value his opinion. I thought he would tell me if I was doing the right thing.'

She looked across at Fenton, whose face was grim. This was dreadful, he was thinking, that all this should have to come out. But he realized that Stacey was acting wisely in being frank with the detective.

Sara Belling had moved across and

held Stacey's arm comfortingly. Levaque glanced at her. 'But what about Mademoiselle Belling?' he said softly. 'Is she not a friend? As your husband's secretary she must have known him well. At least as well as Monsieur Fenton. Could you not have taken her into your confidence?'

'Of course I could,' Stacey said wearily. 'She and I are very good friends. But I felt that perhaps she was too close to my husband, she would react loyally to him. Surely you can understand that?'

Levaque nodded with what might have been an expression of sympathy and understanding.

'I must not distress you by questioning you too much,' he said politely. 'Not now.'

He went to the door and gave some instructions to the police-doctor in the hall as Laking's body was removed and taken down to the ambulance which had arrived and was waiting outside. Levaque had glanced inquiringly at Stacey, as if suggesting she might want to see her husband's body, but she had shaken her head listlessly.

No one in the room spoke. Everyone

seemed to be listening to the murmur of voices in the hall. Dr. Morelle smoked his inevitable Le Sphinx, an aloof, impressive figure. Stacey sat in a chair. Fenton looked at her miserably, knowing what this must be like for her, unable to help. Sara leaned against the corner of a table. She looked up, caught Stacey's eyes, and gave her a warmly sympathetic smile.

When Levaque came back, Fenton stubbed out his cigarette, but to his surprise the detective turned to Sara.

'Was Mr. Laking,' he said to her, 'an unreasonable, a difficult employer?'

'He could be difficult, sometimes,' she said frankly. 'Occasionally he had bursts of violent temper. Lately he'd been rather worse, and I was glad when I knew he was going to see a doctor in London.'

'You saw him when he got back. How did he seem to you?'

'He seemed quite well, but he hadn't much to say.' Sara glanced at Fenton. 'Mr. Laking got here about four o'clock and told me to ring Mr. Fenton and ask him to come over for a drink this evening. Mr. Fenton had a manuscript he wanted

Mr. Laking to have a look at. It's on the writing-desk in there.'

She gave a nod in the direction of the library.

'Go on, please,' Levaque said smoothly.

'I was in the garden getting some flowers,' Sara said, 'when Mr. Fenton arrived and went in.' She went on to describe how she'd gone up to her own room and then had begun wondering about Stacey's continued absence and had decided to go for a walk in the hope of meeting her returning. 'I went into the library and told Mr. Laking. He seemed quite cheerful and told me he was going to read a little more of the manuscript Mr. Fenton had left with him.' She added: 'I didn't meet Mrs. Laking, and after I'd walked for about forty minutes I came home. I found Mr. Fenton and Mrs. Laking with Dr. Morelle. They told me the terrible news.'

She took a deep breath now it was over. Inspector Levaque was silent for a moment, then he said: 'You do not know if Mr. Laking had any enemies here?'

She shook her head. 'Not that I know of.'

Now the detective turned on Dyke Fenton and began questioning him. Still in that casual, almost disinterested manner.

'You see,' Fenton was saying, 'he said he couldn't kill himself because of his life insurance policies, they all contained the usual suicide clause. He said he didn't want Mrs. Laking to suffer financially because of his death. So he suggested I did it. I was to shoot him in the back. Just the same way as he was shot. Only someone else did it.'

Levaque's eyes never left Dyke Fenton's face as he went into the details, describing every minute of that gruesome scene, there in the library. It wasn't until he had finished that he realized he'd forgotten to mention the gun. He waited, expecting Levaque to ask him about that, but the question didn't come.

'What did you do then?' Levaque said.

'Only one thing I could do,' Fenton said. 'Obviously he was out of his mind. I humoured him, pretended to agree. When

I left, my first thought was to find Mrs. Laking and tell her. I reckoned he wouldn't do anything violent so long as he thought I was going to do what he wanted. I phoned round everyone I thought might know where Mrs. Laking was, with no result. So I just waited at my apartment in the hope she would phone me or show up. I hoped she would get in touch with one of the people I'd phoned.' He explained why he'd been afraid to phone Sara, and Levaque gave an understanding nod. 'But when Mrs. Laking did arrive and we got back here, someone had done exactly what he wanted me to do.'

'You think perhaps a burglar killed him?' Levaque said. 'The state of the desk suggests that.'

'I think he was killed by someone who overheard us talking,' Fenton said grimly. 'Or someone he'd already told about his crazy scheme.'

'Someone who knew him, then?'

'I don't know.'

Levaque looked across at Stacey. 'You have many friends in Monte Carlo?'

'A few,' Stacey said slowly. 'Not many. I wouldn't call any of them close friends. I can't believe any one of them would have wished Ian harm.'

Dr. Morelle dragged at his cigarette and said through a cloud of smoke: 'I fancy I may be able to confirm the facts relating to Laking's state of mind. I can get in touch with Sir Trevor Kirkland; it seems he had advised Laking to consult me. We may learn that he harboured thoughts of ending his own life.'

'Thank you, Dr. Morelle,' the detective said politely. 'Though we are not now so very concerned with Mr. Laking's mental state. We have progressed beyond that to a situation where murder seems to have been committed.'

Dr. Morelle gave him the glimmer of a smile. 'I agree that the matter of the man's state of mind has become academic. Except that it will establish whether he was telling Mr. Fenton the truth.'

'Why should he lie about that?' Stacey said.

Dr. Morelle looked at her and then

contemplated the tip of his Le Sphinx. 'Why indeed?' he said.

The others glanced at Levaque, who gave a little shrug as if to say it was of little importance, and then very politely informed Fenton, Stacey and Sara that they must be prepared to hold themselves in readiness to be asked any further questions which might be thought necessary towards a solution of the case. It was impossible to tell what conclusions, if any, he had reached. Fenton and Stacey gloomily watched the detective take his departure. Sara Belling stood unhappily at the door to the hall as Dr. Morelle also prepared to leave. She moved aside and went to Stacey as Fenton said to Dr. Morelle:

'I want to thank you for holding back that letter.'

Dr. Morelle's dark eyes were deep and penetrating. 'You have until tomorrow evening,' he said. 'Then I shall be bound to give it to Levaque.'

16

Dyke Fenton watched Dr. Morelle's tall, gaunt figure silhouetted against the night sky, as with raking strides he went swiftly along the terrace towards the gates, then he slowly closed the door and he stepped back into the hall. He stood there for a moment, with only the eyes of the marble statues upon him, and stared at the chest.

The gun. Who could have known where it was hidden? The bullets were in Laking's body. They would be dug out and then if the gun were found, the police would be able to compare it with those bullets. If they matched, then Laking's gun had fired the fatal shots.

Fenton found Stacey and Sara sitting silently, both looking at the end of their tether. It had been quite a day, he thought grimly.

'Everybody's gone,' he said with assumed cheerfulness. 'Kind of quiet, isn't it?'

They looked at him without answering,

though Sara forced a wan smile to her face. The reality of his position slammed back. He was in a bad spot. Somehow he'd got to find the murderer, and he had hellishly little time in which to do it. How did he start?

'Drink, Dyke?' Stacey said. He nodded and she got up to pour him a generous whisky and soda.

He took the glass from her and gulped back a drink gratefully. 'Looks like Dr. Morelle's on our side, so far,' he said. 'He's not going to hand over that letter until tomorrow evening. That's quite a break.'

'Thank God,' Stacey said. She drew a hand over her face with a desperate kind of weariness, and Fenton's heart went out to her.

'I think he's not half so grim as he looks,' Sara said. 'Rather frightening at a first glance, but maybe that's just something he cultivates. I'm sure he'd help you. After all, we're all English in a foreign country.'

He hardly took in what Sara said, he saw Stacey shiver, there was a dull, beaten look in her eyes.

'What are you going to do, Dyke?' she said anxiously. 'I think Sara's right. I think we should ask Dr. Morelle's help.'

Fenton swirled the whisky round in his glass and peered at it as if he was gazing into a crystal. 'I don't know,' he said at last. 'I'd like to go to him, but I don't feel I can unless I can offer some idea about the real murderer, some lead.'

'My mind's a blank,' Stacey said to him and he saw her shiver again, uncontrollably. She stood up, holding her hands tightly together.

'You've had enough for one day,' he said. 'You'd better try to get some rest.' He turned to Sara, his expression a silent appeal for help.

'I shan't be able to sleep,' Stacey said in a low voice.

'I'll give you a sedative,' Sara said, taking her hand. 'Come on, Stacey. Let's try and take our mind off things together.'

Stacey turned to Dyke Fenton. 'Good night,' she said, and her eyes held his.

'Good night, Stacey,' Dyke said. 'Try not to worry about anything. I'm going back to the apartment to do some

thinking. I'm sure I'll come up with something by morning.'

As soon as they had gone upstairs he went to the library. He switched on the light and he crossed to the desk, which had been tidied up after the police examination. No doubt they'd been through the drawers but presumably even if they'd found anything of interest, such as the Colt automatic, they needn't necessarily have mentioned the fact to him. The manuscript was still on the desk, he noticed absently.

He stood there looking round, recalling the sight of Laking slumped over the desk; remembering the scene between them earlier. He frowned to himself as he tried to think of anything which might point to the whereabouts of the gun. He came to the conclusion that the murderer must have taken it with him.

When he got back to the hall Sara was coming downstairs. If she was curious to know why he had been in the library, she said nothing. He muttered something about having taken a look at the scene of the crime, then he said:

'Is Stacey all right?'

Sara nodded. 'I've given her a sedative.' She shook her head. 'What a dreadful business. I can't believe it's happened.'

He thought she looked pretty near all-in herself. Her eyes were feverishly bright, she was twisting a handkerchief round in her fingers. But she never would break down, he realized. She was one of those who could find an extra reserve of strength, a wry smile, at the worst moments.

'What are we going to do?' she said.

'I don't know yet,' Fenton said. 'It's all happened so suddenly. It seems like some ghastly nightmare.' He said something about getting back to his own place. Then he realized that she wasn't anxious for him to go. He saw that she was shaking a little. 'You've been pretty marvellous,' he said. 'Most girls would have gone off into hysterics.'

It was something to help cheer her up. She looked at him with the hint of a smile. 'I was never one for messy displays of emotion.'

One thing had been troubling him and

he looked at the white-faced young woman who was watching him. 'Sara, will you and Stacey be all right here? Just the two of you in the villa?'

She said quietly: 'Yes, Dyke. Stacey's all right, I'm sure. And it won't bother me. After all, there's always the telephone.'

'Ring me up at once, if you or Stacey feel the need.'

Sara turned abruptly away from Fenton. She seemed to be talking more to herself than him. 'It's bad enough Ian dying in such a ghastly way, but he's dead now and nothing can alter the fact. Now we've got to think about the other things. What's going to happen? The police investigating, and the suspicion?' Her voice trailed away.

Fenton thought he detected a new note of anxiety in her voice. What was Sara getting at? What she was saying had been prompted by something else than Laking's death. Suddenly he asked himself: did she know something that he didn't know? Had she discovered some fact which he had missed? He moved to her and turned her round to face him.

'Sara, what is it?'

'Nothing,' she said quickly, breaking away from him. 'Honestly, it's nothing. I'm just tired, that's all. I'd better go to bed.'

'Sara, you've got to tell me. Do you know something?'

Suddenly she went limp, wiped her hand across her face as if wiping away an evil cloud.

'Dyke, I'm afraid,' she said.

'But you said you'd be all right here,' Fenton said.

'It's not that. I'm not afraid of the villa, or of being alone with Stacey.'

'What is it, then?'

She moved closer, her fingers dug into his arm.

'Don't you see,' she said. 'I'm afraid for Stacey.'

Dyke Fenton stared at her. Her words stung him, through the heaviness of fatigue which had begun to envelop him. What did she mean? Surely Stacey was in no danger. Laking was dead now.

'What are you saying?' he asked harshly. 'Why are you afraid for her?'

'The suspicion,' Sara said. 'The questions.' She broke off. 'I can't help

thinking,' she said in a low voice. 'I know it's awful, but I can't help remembering.'

Fenton was disturbed. Sara was trying to tell him something. Something that concerned Stacey. He had to get it out of her, he had to know, even if it was bad. He gripped her shoulder and Sara brought her eyes up to his.

'What is it you can't help thinking?' he said. 'You've remembered something, is that it? Something to do with Stacey?'

She took a deep breath. 'I can tell you, Dyke, because I know you won't lose your head. It's just that, living so close to Ian and Stacey, I heard things. I couldn't help it. And now this awful thing has happened it, it makes you wonder all kinds of things. You understand?'

He felt a stab of pain, the twisting knife of anguish. He knew now what Sara was hinting at. It was crazy. But he had to let her say it.

'You'd better go on, tell me.'

'It was just before Ian went to London,' Sara said in a low voice. 'There was a terrible row between him and Stacey.'

'There's nothing in that,' Fenton said.

'It's a wonder she kept as calm as she did. Anyway,' and he grinned wryly, 'husbands and wives have to have rows, let off steam, it's a kind of safety valve.'

'But this was different.'

'How was it so different?'

'It was the night before he left for London. He stormed out of Stacey's room. I could hear both their voices. They were both furious. And I heard — '

'What did you hear?' Fenton said raspingly.

'I heard her tell him he ought to be shot.'

Fenton winced. So that was it. It was hard to imagine Stacey talking like that. But she'd been near the end of her tether. Nearer than any of them had realized. She could have said it without meaning it. She could never have done it.

'Did you hear what he said?'

'I couldn't help it. He was shouting so loud. He said something like: 'Fine, fine, here's a gun, why don't you use it?' Then I heard her door slam shut and a few seconds later I heard him go into his own room. I don't know if he actually had a

gun. I didn't hear anything else.'

Sara looked up at Dyke Fenton with frightened eyes. 'And now he's dead, and the gun has disappeared from where you hid it. Oh, Dyke, don't you see? I know it's a terrible thing even to think about, but I can't help it.'

'You're tired,' Fenton said levelly. 'You've been through a lot tonight and you're all confused.'

That was it, he told himself. Sara was distraught and her mind would seize on any suspicious incident. The first thing it had thrown up was the threatening scene she had overheard, and the talk about the gun. It meant nothing. In normal circumstances she'd never even have remembered it.

He must get it into perspective in Sara's mind. If she started to dwell on it she'd soon magnify it out of all proportion. Probably she'd started already.

'I'm sure you can forget it, Sara,' he said. 'It's just a coincidence the gun being mentioned. She was overwrought and you know it's easy to say anything when you're in that state. Anything cruel, that

hurts. And he was half out of his mind.'

Sara nodded, but her face was clouded. 'Of course you're right,' she said. 'I mustn't think about it. I only told you because I needed someone to reassure me. I promise you I'll forget it.'

'You need sleep,' Fenton said. 'I do, too. You're sure you'll be all right?'

'I'm all right now,' she said. She seemed to be her own cool self again. He had reassured her, by the way he had taken what she'd told him. 'And you won't worry about what I told you?' he heard her say.

'I've already forgotten it,' he said, and watched her go upstairs. She didn't look back.

17

Dyke Fenton let himself out of the villa and made his way through the garden to the road. The scent of the flowers, the beauty of the night about him and the distant murmur of the sea mocked him. He took in the gleam of lights, the sound of music somewhere in the distance without being aware that they existed. He might have been anywhere on earth but Monte Carlo, with its glamour and allure which had charmed him.

He'd lied to Sara. He hadn't forgotten what she said. He couldn't forget it. The scene she had recalled was so painfully easy to imagine. But he decided that Sara must have got it wrong. Stacey could never threaten anyone, however upset she was. But how could Sara be wrong, he argued? If their voices were raised she couldn't help over-hearing them.

Hands thrust deep into his pockets, Dyke Fenton's thoughts struggled to

shape a sane picture that would eliminate the nagging hint of suspicion. In a dark corner of his mind a morsel of doubt fed on that suspicion like a rat on garbage.

Stacey had admitted to him that her life with Ian was intolerable. Suppose she had overheard that macabre scene between him and Laking? He stopped and tried to thrust the crazy idea out of his mind. But suppose she had acted on Laking's crazy plan?

It was despicable of him even to waste a minute on the idea. Yet the circumstances were peculiar. Stacey had been away all day. She had been out to lunch, and that he had confirmed, when he had phoned round for her earlier on, when he had wanted to contact her so urgently. But what of the afternoon? On her own admission she had been alone, making up her mind about leaving Ian.

Or so she had said. There was no-one to corroborate her story. Where had she been before she came to his apartment? Suppose she had in fact returned to the Villa des Fleurs just when Laking was outlining his plan in the library? Suppose

she had been outside the french windows and heard every word, and in some way seen him or guessed at it, hide the gun in the chest. Suppose — ?

For God's sake stop this ghastly supposing, he told himself. He swung into the street entrance to his apartment, realizing sickeningly that he was beginning to suspect Stacey, that he couldn't drive that suspicion from his brain.

He had only to remember her desperate anxiety for him, he tried to tell himself now, when Dr. Morelle had read out Laking's letter. He had only to remind himself of the unspoken bond of affection which existed between them. Stacey was wonderful, he knew as well as he knew himself, a generous woman, who would be quite incapable of doing harm to anyone.

He felt ashamed, angry with himself for allowing his faith in Stacey to sag. Even suppose she had told Ian he deserved to be shot, that wasn't a threat. She wasn't the threatening type. It was natural for Sara to remember the incident, to connect it with Laking's death. But it was

just a coincidence. Probably Stacey would tell him of the row, herself, tomorrow. It was disloyal and wicked to mark her up as a suspect.

With a tremendous effort of will he pushed the whole matter out of his mind.

He let himself into his apartment, switched on the lights, and found himself staring out of the window as he had done earlier. Now the sky was velvet, spattered with stars. It seemed incredible to him that so much could have happened in the space of those few, brief hours. He'd better go to bed. There was nothing more he could do that night. Depression had set in, it was reaction after the excitement and he felt weary. A few hours' sleep would make all the difference. He would see the whole hideous problem in a new light when he awoke in the morning.

He took a warm shower, slipped into pyjamas and back in the bedroom he stood eyeing his divan bed. It ought to look comfortable. But it didn't tonight. He felt too taut and restless to sleep. He knew he would lie there, thinking. Thinking round and round the same

theme. He'd lie there in the dark and every thought in his mind would loom big and distorted. It'd be a nightmare without even going to sleep.

He went back to the sitting-room and lit a cigarette. He was in a tight spot. And he was alone. He couldn't even approach Dr. Morelle, he'd nothing to offer him.

Before this time tomorrow Levaque would have Laking's letter. The letter that damned Dyke Fenton as a cold-blooded killer, who had killed the husband of the woman with whom he was infatuated. Dr. Morelle had given him a breathing space, given him time to clear himself. But no help. Dyke realized he'd got to make it on his own. But how? Which way did he go from here?

He went over to the window. Below the rich, shimmering lights of Monte Carlo winked back at him through the darkness. But now there was no warmth, no comfort in their glow. From a garden there stole to him the scents of mimosa and cyclamen, irises, primulas and daturas and a dozen other flowers; the musical splash-splash of a fountain hung

on the soft breeze that drifted in gently from the Mediterranean. Beyond the sumptuous villas lay the Casino and the Sporting Club, where in the haze of cigar-smoke and expensive perfumes gamblers risked their millions of francs as they'd worked it out by the stars, or mathematics, according to their fancy; elegant men and women, the millionaires and celebrities known to all the world, danced to famous dance-orchestras or dined and drank from their magnums of champagne and flirted and gossiped.

Dyke Fenton had amused himself playing the tables and he made out not too badly, the wheel of fortune had run his way. But this was a different, a more deadly game of chance he had found himself caught up in tonight. A game in which from the very first setting up of the chips the wheel had been loaded against him.

Dyke Fenton turned back into the room, his hands clenched, the sweat had begun to break out on his brow. Somehow he'd got to find the murderer. Or else.

18

It is difficult to feel chilled in Monte Carlo but Miss Frayle felt frozen almost stiff with disbelieving horror. 'I assure you that I booked the room for two weeks from the fifth.' In her frustration she beat her hand on the reception-desk.

The *pension* proprietor shut his eyes as if infinitely weary and shook his head. '*Non, mademoiselle,*' he said, pronouncing each word with the utmost care. 'When you telephoned you said that you would be arriving on the twentieth.'

'I said *le cinq.*'

'You said *le vingt.*'

A man and a woman staying at the little *pension* passed through the hall. They paused just outside the doorway in the cobbled road as if listening to the discussion between Miss Frayle and the plump little man. Seeing their shadows stretched across the sunlit pavement the man looked towards them and raised his

eyes heavenwards as if to show how patient he was being.

'Mademoiselle,' he said, 'there is no point in continuing the discussion. The mistake arose, no doubt, because the words *cinq* and *vignt* can sound identical over the telephone. If it were possible to accommodate you I should be happy to do so. But as I told you, I have no room vacant until the twentieth.'

Miss Frayle didn't know what to do. She stared at her luggage, then looked hopelessly round the hall. An archway at the back opened on to an inner courtyard. It looked so romantic she would gladly have slept on the circular bench which had been placed round one of the orange trees growing there. Staircases built along the outside of the building led up from the paved yardway to the rooms on the second floor.

Miss Frayle sighed. Ever since she had heard about the place from a friend in Paris she had imagined herself climbing the staircase to her room. The room she had booked had a balcony at the front which looked across to the harbour and

the Mediterranean. From it, she had been told, she could see the mountains which ranged along the coastline to Italy. She sighed again. She had planned to sit every morning on the balcony, taking her breakfast and admiring the view.

The door of one of the ground-floor rooms opened and a man emerged carrying a suitcase. At the sight of him Miss Frayle's spirits rose, she turned quickly to the proprietor but before she could speak he raised his hands above his head and waved them impatiently.

'Mademoiselle, I am sorry. That room is booked. I have told you, I have no vacancies. I regret the mistake, but it is not my fault.'

'All right, all right,' she said huffily. 'We won't go through all that again.'

He wiped a plump hand across his face, thankful to have at last persuaded the English mademoiselle that he could not help her.

'I suppose you don't know any other hotel I could try?'

Mon Dieu, he thought, would she never go away? He opened his mouth to

give a short reply, then softened. Really, she looked a trifle pathetic, standing there with her suitcases.

'Look here,' he said. 'If you wish you may leave your cases here while you try for another place. It is very hot, and you will get tired carrying them with you.' He shrugged. 'I don't think you have much prospect of finding a good room in this quarter. It might be best to go to the new part of the town. One of the big hotels could doubtless accommodate you.'

Rather subdued now, Miss Frayle thanked him and went across the hall. At the doorway she suddenly brightened and turned back. 'Of course if anything happens and you do get a vacancy, you'll let me have first chance, won't you?'

The man's benevolent smile vanished. He shut his eyes and called upon the saints in heaven to help him in his trials. Miss Frayle stepped quickly through the door of the little white hotel. She was not anxious to hear his reply.

Making her way dismally down the sloping terrace she thought: *cinq, vingt,* there wouldn't have been this trouble if

I'd sent a written confirmation. But he told me not to trouble. It's all his fault.

She tried at the first hotel she came to, but the large woman at reception shook her head. She tried again at the next hotel she came to, and again, but each time she was turned away with the same answer.

'I'm sorry, mademoiselle. If you had come earlier in the season, or even later, I'd have been able to help you. But now I am completely booked up.'

Oh dear, Miss Frayle thought, after the tenth hotel. I'm in for a long walk. A good job I slept on the train.

Her train had left the Gare de Lyons just after eight o'clock the previous evening. She had spent the evening in a frenzy of packing, she had checked her suitcases at least three times. Finally she crammed in a few extra things, just in case they might be needed. Madame Grimault had watched her with obvious amusement. After an hour of it she had said: 'Really, Miss Frayle, you are not usually so flustered. Is this holiday so important to you? Are you perhaps meeting a friend?'

Miss Frayle's blush was sufficient answer. 'Well, I'm not sure. Perhaps I might,' she had said, stammering.

Madame Grimault had smiled knowingly. 'In that case I understand. I will make you some coffee.'

Miss Frayle had left the Samurai sword behind, after all.

The Gare de Lyons had been its usual dingy, bustling noisy self. Miss Frayle had booked a couchette on the train and because she had followed her usual practice of getting to the station far too early, she had time to settle back and watch the activity.

Her carriage slowly filled up. Miss Frayle wondered again why French people always seemed so hungry in trains. As soon as the train left the station she was banged in the ear by the end of a baguette which her neighbour was extricating from a basket. The woman chopped it into three pieces, cut each piece straight along the middle and inserted thick wedges of paté. Her husband opened a bottle of wine and they settled back to enjoy the meal, completely

oblivious of their neighbours.

The paté smelt strongly of garlic. Miss Frayle wrinkled her nose, and had eyed the couple resentfully. They were both very dark, and short and stocky in type. Corsicans, she decided.

Before long Miss Frayle had got into conversation with the woman who sat opposite to her. She was a schoolteacher from Lyons, Miss Frayle learned, who spoke excellent English, and she was interested to find that Miss Frayle came from London. Did Miss Frayle like Paris? She had nodded enthusiastically. Yes, she had grown to love Paris during the past few months. This made her an immediate success with everybody in the carriage. Someone offered her a light rug so that she could sleep more comfortably, the man she had decided was Corsican, and who turned out to be a real Parisian, as was his wife, offered her a drink of wine, and his wife tried to force a paté sandwich on her. Miss Frayle accepted the rug but refused the food. She wanted, she said, to eat in the restaurant-car. She always enjoyed meals on trains.

The schoolteacher had joined her and they chattered happily together during the four-course meal. Miss Frayle drank rather more wine than she was accustomed to and as she had returned to the compartment after the meal she was concerned to find that she felt slightly tipsy. She settled down on her couchette and allowed herself to sink into a comfortable daze.

Travelling through a foreign country at night, she thought dreamily, was the most exciting thing in the world. The noise and the cries at the railway-stations sounded so romantic, so strange. Even the tang of the countryside, she thought, as she had fallen asleep, was new and wonderful.

She had slept soundly and when she awoke the train was already steaming out of Avignon. She lay for a while in that blissful state between sleep and waking, then at last roused herself and sat up.

What she saw when she looked out of the window had made her gasp. 'Why,' she said aloud, 'it's like a gigantic Van Gogh painting.' Cypress and olive trees stood out almost black against the deep

reddish-blue of the early morning sky. The sun, shining across a belt of trees, showed them a wonderful deep shining green.

This was Van Gogh's part of the world, the schoolteacher had told her with a proud smile. 'This is where he came towards the end of his life. You see how wrong people are who suppose he painted like that because he was mad.'

It was the end of Miss Frayle's sleep. She had sat with her nose glued to the window, terrified of missing something. The Parisian couple disembarked at Marseilles. They were to catch a boat to a little Corsican place where they always went for a holiday. The husband was grumbling about Marseilles and the long hill down from the station to the harbour. His wife shrugged and turned to Miss Frayle. 'You should spend a day in Marseilles, Mademoiselle. It is a most picturesque town, with the Moroccans and Arabs walking about in their national dress. And the fish you can buy in the harbour, ah, they are superb.'

The man and his wife had scrambled

off the train with their mountain of baskets and cases. Miss Frayle waved, feeling quite sad to see them go, then she went along to the restaurant car for breakfast.

She was almost too excited to eat. From one side of the train she saw mountainous scenery, from the other, the Mediterranean, with beaches like strips of silver against the intense blue of sea and sky.

I've never seen anything like it, Miss Frayle told herself. No wonder they call it the Côte d'Azur.

The train went through Cannes and Nice, both speckled with yellow and white buildings which glinted in the morning sunlight. 'Not long now before you can see Monte Carlo,' the schoolteacher had said to her and soon she was pointing through the window. 'There it is.'

The tiny principality of Monaco lay in a three-sided well, formed by the mountains which rose away from it. On the fourth side the sea stretched away to the horizon.

Miss Frayle had started to muse romantically about Princess Grace and Prince Ranier. Their story had been like a fairytale, she told herself. She looked eagerly for a glimpse of the palace and thought that she caught a sight of it.

This was going to be a wonderful holiday, she had thought. If only she could meet that certain someone she hoped to meet, it would be the most exciting holiday of her life.

And here she was in Monte Carlo, the place of her dreams, without a roof over her head. Miss Frayle was jerked back from her day-dreaming by the feel of the warm stones under her shoes. The hotel proprietor had been right. It was hot work walking round the city.

She turned a corner and chanced across a market where there was such a jumble of produce that she was fleetingly reminded of the Marché aux Puces in Paris. Trinkets, souvenirs, clothes, umbrellas, handbags, beach sandals, and fruit, she had never seen such fruit. Stalls were piled high with grapes, oranges, greengages, peaches, melons. Her mouth watered.

'Mademoiselle,' a voice chanted. '*Regardez les pêches.*'

'You look sad, mademoiselle,' another voice called. 'Have you lost all your money at the Casino?'

She joined in the laughter and bought some peaches. They were good, she found, biting into their velvety skins and gasping as the sweet juice dribbled down her chin.

I suppose I ought to have a look at the Casino, she thought. Maybe if I was lucky and won something, I might be able to afford to stay at one of the big hotels. She felt a first thrill of excitement. She had never gambled in her life, perhaps she would have beginner's luck.

She began wandering away from the old town and along the Boulevard des Moulins towards the Casino. She heard again Madame Grimault's voice explaining some of the history of Monaco, how the place had been poor and almost unknown until the mid-eighteen-fifties, its only connection with France an almost insurmountable cart-track. And then a tremendous anti-gambling campaign had

surged through the Continent. Gambling was banned in Paris, croupiers found themselves looking for new territories and Prince Charles Albert of Monaco gave permission for Monte Carlo to set up a gambling-house, and the frustrated gamblers had swarmed over the mountains and almost overnight Monte Carlo was made.

Now, Miss Frayle's eyes widened behind their horn-rims when the Casino came into view. It looked for all the world like a Christmas-cake, she thought, all covered with white icing. The gardens that fronted the Casino were splashed with vivid summer flowers. The whole thing was like something out of a colour film.

Miss Frayle began to experience a decidedly fluttery and nervous feeling even at the prospect of risking a small amount of money in the gaming rooms. But she hoped she would be able to pluck up courage later to try her luck. She envisaged herself putting off the dangerous moment by wandering round, studying the people at the various tables.

Finally she would go boldly forward, she assured herself. She would hazard only a few francs. To start with at any rate. In her imagination she could picture herself staring in awed wonder at the white and gold decoration of the gambling *salon*, with its crystal chandeliers shimmering over her head, she could hear the well-known phrases: '*Faites vos jeux, messieurs, mesdames . . . les jeux sont faits. Rien ne va plus.*'

She brought her thoughts back to the present and the job of finding herself a room. Then her attention was distracted by the white-stone cathedral of St. Nicholas. Standing in the arched doorway she looked over a fringe of palms to the Mediterranean. It was true, from almost anywhere in Monte Carlo could be seen wonderful landscapes of mountains and sea.

If only she could meet that certain someone she had hoped to meet, she thought again, and with mounting excitement she drifted on in the glorious sunshine, trying to concentrate on finding that blessed hotel room. She stood

outside the Musée Oceanique, feeling a little hot now and wondering how cool it would be inside. She would have to go to one of the big hotels and book a room for the night, at any rate, she was deciding. The expense couldn't be helped.

And then, a little dazed, as she left the sunshine for the cool shadows of the aquarium she was attracted by a group of people gazing down at something in the floor. She inched her way into the group and her eyes widened in amazement as she saw the glass panel at her feet. She was looking right down into the Mediterranean.

This is quite marvellous, she thought. I've never seen anything like this in my life.

The walls of the aquarium were lined with tanks, and contained an immense collection of fishes. Miss Frayle went round staring at them, almost hypnotized by the various fish which eyed her from behind the glass. The baby octopuses made her shiver, they looked decidedly slimy, but the little sea-horses were highly entertaining. They were so graceful as

they swam and curvetted in the water, anchoring themselves around the sea-plants by their tails.

As for the flat-fish, she had never seen so many different colours. Some as blue as the Mediterranean, others a deep blood-red, or yellow, or purply-brown. Wonderful, fascinating, she kept saying to herself.

Until she saw the ray.

It was resting in the water with its back turned to the onlookers when Miss Frayle approached. Two teenage boys were gaping at it.

'Ugly great thing,' one of them said with a pronounced American accent. The other agreed.

Miss Frayle idly wondered what sort of face the thing might possess and decided to attract its attention. She tapped on the glass of its tank. Disturbed by the vibrations the ray turned swiftly to see Miss Frayle peering inquisitively at it.

Its horrid bulging eyes stared directly into her own eyes blinking behind the horn-rims. Then it charged straight for her. As it shot closer the special

magnifying-glass of the tank made it look enormous, appalling.

In that horrifying moment Miss Frayle knew it was going to burst out at her through the glass.

She opened her mouth and screamed.

19

The scream rang through the long shadowy gallery. Dr. Morelle, who had been deep in thought, spun round. His musings upon the events the previous night at the Villa des Fleurs shattered. He had put in a long-distance telephone call to London and talked at some length, as a result of which he had made another phone-call, this time to the Monte Carlo police-office. It was from there that he had just come, after a chat with Levaque. From the Frenchman he had learned one or two items of interest: the calibre of the bullets which had smashed into Laking's body, and the approximate time of death, which corroborated in that respect at any rate the story told by the other occupants of the Villa des Fleurs, and the young man named Fenton. Dr. Morelle had also learned that the daily servant who worked for the Lakings had left at the usual time at about five p.m., while Laking was alive.

This servant, a middle-aged woman from the other side of Monaco, had been interviewed by Levaque, but he had gained nothing fresh from her. He glanced ahead now at what seemed to be the point of disturbance in the aquarium, then saw against the greenish light of the glass fish tanks, a small excited group, all gesticulating energetically.

Dr. Morelle made his way quickly towards the group. The high-pitched feminine voice which was using the French language so precisely and with a strong English accent sounded somewhat familiar to his ears, but he concluded they must be playing him tricks. Perhaps some oddity caused by human voices echoing against the glass tanks, he thought.

'What is happening?' he said in French as he reached the noisy group, which included two teenage boys talking in American accents. Everyone began to speak at once but the tall, authoritative figure bearing down on them forced them to give way.

So his hearing hadn't been playing him tricks, after all, Dr. Morelle thought, as he

encountered the familiar slim figure with the soft fair hair and wide frightened eyes behind their horn-rims. With a yelp of delighted amazement she rushed forward with outstretched arms.

'Dr. Morelle, how simply marvellous. You're the last person I expected to find here, but you've come just in time.'

'In time for what, my dear Miss Frayle?'

She fluttered. 'Oh, to explain what happened.' She indicated the several men and the two boys who were goggling at her and Dr. Morelle.

His keen gaze fastened on her with such intensity that she blushed. 'Just what was it made you cry out?'

'I couldn't help it,' she said, very shame-faced. 'I was frightened.'

He threw a glance round the group, who were beginning to drift away. Then he followed Miss Frayle's wild look at the fish-tank which contained the fish which had scared her out of her wits. 'I was just trying to explain to them it was that horrible monster that frightened me.'

Dr. Morelle's expression was typically

unsympathetic, Miss Frayle noted with dismay. 'Aren't you behaving a trifle absurdly?' he said in those icy tones she had known so well in the not-so-distant past. 'It is quite apparent that it could not possibly harm you, even if it wished to, which is doubtful.'

He turned away from her to those who remained watching the scene with amused curiosity. He spoke to them in fluent French, explaining the misunderstanding. Miss Frayle considerably embarrassed, saw their smiles and heard the laughing comments they made as they turned away. The two American boys eyed her with pitying grins as they moved off, discussing her stupidity in their loud, uninhibited accents.

She turned her attention to the giant ugly fish that had caused all the trouble. It was close to the window of the tank, a great flat fish with wicked bulging eyes and a wide mouth which it slowly opened and closed. Each side of its body flapped slowly up and down like the giant wings of a bird in slow motion.

'That's what frightened me,' Miss Frayle said.

'A specimen, it would appear, of the elasmobranch family Rajidae,' Dr. Morelle said. 'Quite an interesting specimen,' studying it intently.

'I only tried to attract its attention by tapping on the glass. It swam towards me, its eyes seemed to be staring right into mine, and then suddenly it seemed to charge.' She gave a nervous giggle. 'It looked so terribly big and ferocious I thought it was going to burst right through the glass. That was when I screamed.'

'It was as curious to look at you as you were to look at it,' Dr. Morelle said. 'And it seems to have got the best of the encounter.' Miss Frayle frowned at him a little, she didn't quite like the way in which he was regarding her. As if he was comparing her with that horrible fish, and perhaps not even to her advantage. 'The glass used in these windows magnifies the fish,' he was saying, 'and makes them look a good deal bigger than they really are.' He turned back to her and eyed her

sombrely. 'But what are you doing in Monte Carlo, Miss Frayle? I thought you were engrossed in your studies in Paris.'

'I am,' she said earnestly. 'But everyone needs a holiday. And I thought I'd take the opportunity of having a look at Monte Carlo. After all, it's supposed to be such a fabulous place. I wanted to see it for myself.' She added extremely unconvincingly: 'Of course I had no idea I should run into you here, Dr. Morelle.'

She found herself blushing furiously, and knew at once that he knew she was lying. A trace of a smile crossed his face, and she knew that he was aware that she knew she was lying. She hadn't been in his company five minutes before she was feeling confused and overcome by a devastating sense of his superiority and omnipotence. Why on earth had she come to this place with these horrid fish? He took her by the arm and urged her along past the fish-tanks. 'Since you are on holiday, hadn't you better make the most of the Mediterranean sun?'

He led her out of the aquarium and through the flamboyant colour of the

tropical gardens to a café with tables outside under gaily-coloured sunshades. Dr. Morelle ordered a bottle of white Lacrima Christi and Miss Frayle began to recover her poise and cheer up. She sipped her glass of wine which was deliciously refreshing, and stared rapturously around her. This, she thought happily, was after all, the longed-for outcome of her visit to Monte Carlo. Why not admit it to herself, if not to him, and enjoy it while she could? Sitting at a café table with Dr. Morelle, just the two of them. It was perfect. All the same she avoided Dr. Morelle's eyes.

The scene was like something out of a highly-coloured musical comedy, she thought. Fashionably-dressed people at the other tables, birds singing their heads off all around, everywhere a riot of colour, and always in the background, like a theatre backdrop, the deep blue of sea and sky.

After a few minutes she stole a glance at Dr. Morelle. He was lighting one of his inevitable Le Sphinx and for a moment she was able to study his face. He had not

changed at all, perhaps he looked a trifle more sardonic, that was all.

It was as if she had left his employment only the day before, to embark on her studies at the Sorbonne. She wondered wistfully if he had missed her. Even if he had, she knew he would never admit the fact. How wonderful it would be, to spend a few lazy days, just the two of them, sipping wine, swimming in the Mediterranean, enjoying one another's company, just like any other holiday-makers. Nothing could be more romantic to contemplate. But it was a dream. Dr. Morelle had no time for dreams of that kind. Only for work. All this was wasted on him.

All the same she began to feel glad she had come. And what a wonderful coincidence it had been, meeting him in the aquarium like that. She had spent such a lot of time wondering how she was going to contrive a meeting, without him becoming suspicious. And now here they were, together. It was too good to be true.

Dr. Morelle leaned forward. 'I hope you are enjoying your wine,' he said.

'It's very nice,' she said, trying to sound as if she'd come to know something about wines as a result of living in France. She reached for her glass. 'It's so lovely here, I was day-dreaming.'

'That was inclined to be one of your failings,' he said, then he raised his glass, a glint of humour in his eyes. 'Here's to your holiday.'

'Thank you, Dr. Morelle,' she said. 'I'm so looking forward to it, but I'm sure you're hard at work.'

'I haven't done nearly enough work,' he said regretfully. 'I came here to find peace and solitude, but even in such a place as this events impose themselves and distract me.'

'I do hope you don't mean me, Dr. Morelle,' she said, with a look of pique, which he failed to notice, however, his gaze had fixed somewhere beyond her shoulder.

'Not at all, my dear Miss Frayle. How long have you been in Monte Carlo?'

'I only got here this morning,' she said, suddenly downcast as she remembered that she had not yet found a hotel. 'I

caught the night train from Paris.'

Dr. Morelle watched a cloud of smoke from his Le Sphinx fade on the warm air, then he looked at her curiously. 'You arrived this morning and I find you in that place before lunch? What is the attraction? I had no idea you were so interested in aquaria species. Can it be that you have been withholding the knowledge of some secret obsession all this time?'

He was laughing at her. She said defensively: 'Oh, I just found myself there. I felt a bit depressed and I was wandering around — '

'You were suffering from depression within an hour of your arrival in Monte Carlo? It is evident that something must have gone amiss with your plans.'

'I have had a bit of a let-down,' she said reluctantly. 'A mistake over my hotel-room.'

She thought she detected a sudden odd glint in his narrowed eyes, as he leaned back and contemplated her over the rim of his glass. What was it, she wondered that had aroused his interest? He said

nothing and she went on talking.

'You see, I booked a room by telephone from Paris. It was a little hotel someone had told me about. But when I got here this morning the man said there's been a mistake, and it was already occupied, the room I'd booked, I mean. He had nothing else to offer and it isn't easy to find a place at a reasonable price. So I was wandering around, wondering what I could do.'

Dr. Morelle seemed to be concentrating all his attention in his glass of wine. 'So you've nowhere to go,' he said thoughtfully.

Miss Frayle nodded and sipped her wine. 'I'll have to find somewhere before tonight, even if it's expensive.' She said, a little hopelessly: 'I suppose you wouldn't know of somewhere, Dr. Morelle?'

'I am sure we should be able to find you suitable accommodation somewhere,' Dr. Morelle said. He looked at her suddenly. 'There is however one other possibility.' Now a hint of a smile hovered at the corners of his chiselled mouth. Then he said with elaborate casualness:

'That is, you might care to stay at the Villa Midnight? I am sure the Comtesse would raise no objection.' He explained briefly how it was that he came to be in occupation at the Villa Midnight.

Miss Frayle's face lit up, her eyes sparkled. 'Dr. Morelle, that would be marvellous,' she said. 'If it wouldn't bother you, or interfere with your work. I'd promise not to make myself a nuisance.'

Then she had a mental picture of the woman whose villa it was. A glamorous, elegant, svelte creature, she was sure. And then she wondered if it was the same woman who'd given him that slim, gold cigarette-case he always used? She was a French countess, or was she Italian? 'I don't know how to thank you,' she heard herself say automatically. 'I'm sure it'll be lovely.' She was trying to recall what marvellous thing Dr. Morelle had done for the countess, or comtesse, or whatever she was, which had caused her to reward him with the cigarette-case. Saved her from a blackmailer, or something.

Miss Frayle raised her glass, then

paused as Dr. Morelle went on speaking. 'It has occurred to me,' he was saying, 'that there is a little typing and shorthand which I'm sure you wouldn't mind in the least doing for me, Miss Frayle. So our meeting is fortunate from both our points of view. You might be able to give me a certain amount of assistance on this work I'm occupied with at the moment. You would find it most interesting and stimulating, I feel positive.'

Miss Frayle said nothing, and her wine-glass hid her expression of growing dismay and disappointment.

20

It was very dark. Like a long tunnel the walls of which were shrouded in a clinging mist. He was moving unsteadily forward, driven on by some irresistible urge, but not knowing where he was going, or what was the object of his journey, what lay beyond the misty darkness.

Voices, sometimes near sometimes a great way off, sounded in his ears, and their strange echoes reverberated all about him. He reached out like a blind man, but there was no-one there. The mist was swirling now and he could see a face in front of him. A smiling, beautiful face. One he knew. It was Stacey. And she was beckoning.

The voices had faded and the silence was broken by the dripping of water which slowly turned to the far-off murmur of the sea. He couldn't seem to reach Stacey. She was out there on the

edge of the sea, silhouetted against a pale horizon. Every step he took towards her seemed to take her further away. But always her curving hand was extended towards him, coldly luminous, beckoning him on.

The darkness faded and suddenly he was close to her, but even now she seemed strange and distant. Neither of them spoke. But there was an unspoken bond between them, invisible, unbreakable. She led him across a stretch of sand which clung to his feet to a crumbling place which reminded him of another place he'd known, only he couldn't recall where it was. Then he knew that they were outside the Villa des Fleurs. Stacey turned her back on him and pressed the doorbell. It began to ring, distant at first, then louder, nearer, more insistent.

Stacey swung back to him, came closer. Her face was suddenly distorted, ugly, grinning. All at once he saw it wasn't her face at all, but the face of Ian Laking.

Dyke Fenton drew back from the figure with a muffled scream. Then he opened his eyes and found himself on the floor

beside his divan. The struggle to escape from the nightmare had thrown him out of bed. Sunlight was filtering through the blind but the bell he had heard in his dream was still ringing. As he staggered to his feet he realized it was the telephone in the sitting-room. He glanced at his wrist-watch. It was approaching eleven-thirty. He stared at the time foolishly. His watch must have stopped last night. It couldn't be as late as this in the morning. Yet he could hear the watch still ticking.

Dyke Fenton was in a cold sweat. The memory of the nightmare was still so vivid he could hardly believe it had not been real. But nightmare or not, the message, he thought, had been clear enough. Laking was laughing at him. Wherever the dead man was, and whoever had obliged him in his grisly plan, Laking had the laugh on him now.

In the sitting-room, the telephone continuing to jangle insistently, he tried to bring his blurred gaze into focus on the travelling clock by the telephone. It showed nearly eleven-thirty, too. He'd slept half the morning through. What

time had it been when he got back from his aimless, miserable walk which he had found himself taking last night?

He had tried desperately to catch some sleep, but it had been no use. In the end he'd got up and dressed again and wandered out into the street. He supposed he'd walked and walked himself into a state of exhaustion, he had no clear recollection of going back to his apartment and bed. It must have been the early hours of the morning. The first light of dawn had been in the sky when he let himself in, he seemed to recall. He must have fallen asleep finally from sheer physical exhaustion, but even that had not stopped his mind from conjuring up ghastly nightmares while he slept. And now he was awake the pictures were still there, flashing across his mind in a crazy pattern like the lights of the Casino.

Fenton sat down heavily and stared at the telephone. Was it that damned detective, Levaque? Did the police want him for questioning again? He picked the instrument up and held it to his ear with an effort.

'Dyke, this is Stacey. Are you all right?'

Relief flooded through him at the sound of her voice. He realized how scared he was of talking to the police. 'I'm all right,' he said. 'A bit second-hand, but that's my own fault, I've been walking around the houses most of the night.' She commiserated with him. 'I'm okay,' he said. 'But you, Stacey? Did the sedative give you a good night?'

'Not too bad,' she said. 'Only I feel as if I'm doped. Sara let me sleep late, but I wish she hadn't. I'm still in my room, and now the police have called again.'

He caught the knife-edge of panic in her voice. 'Is it Levaque?' he said, the image of the blue-chinned, casual-mannered Frenchman in his mind's eye.

'Yes,' she said. 'Sara's talking to him at the moment. I saw him and his stooge coming through the garden. Oh, Dyke,' she said suddenly, a catch in her tone, 'I'm afraid.'

'Nothing to worry about,' he said automatically. 'He probably only wants to ask a few more routine questions. Something he forgot last night.'

'But why should he be back so soon, if he doesn't think we know more than we've already told him?'

'They're professional naggers, it's their job,' he said lightly. He had to give her the impression it was all routine stuff, he knew all about it. Stacey mustn't lose her head. 'They'll keep on coming round for cosy chats, hinting at this, asking about that. It's the way they operate, especially when the poor bastards haven't got a clue, and know it.' He forced a note of confidence into his voice. 'Anyway you and I haven't anything to fear, Stacey. We're in the clear, both of us, and you can bet this chap Levaque knows it, only he's got to keep at us until something else comes up, which it will. Then he'll be on to it and that'll let us out.'

'You sound so cool and unruffled about it,' she said despairingly. 'But I can't help wishing we could do something ourselves, before Dr. Morelle hands that letter over to the police.'

You can say that again, he thought

desperately as a rush of apprehensive recollections swept over his sleep-muddled mind. That blasted letter. 'I know,' he said to Stacey, still trying to sound relaxed on it. 'That's what I was thinking about all last night when I couldn't sleep. It seems to me there's only one thing for me.'

He heard Stacey draw in her breath sharply. Then she said: 'What, Dyke?'

'Go to Dr. Morelle,' he said. 'And leave it all to him.'

'I suppose so, Dyke. But if only we knew he was on our side.' There was that mingling of fear and horror in her voice. Then she spoke quickly in a rush of words. 'Don't go to him yet. Wait until I've talked to Levaque. I might find out what the blessed man knows, if he does know anything more since last night. Perhaps I might learn just a few more facts you could give Dr. Morelle. Wait a bit longer, Dyke. I'l ring you as soon as he's gone. Then you can come round and we'll talk.'

'All right,' he said. 'I'll wait here until you ring.'

201

Dyke Fenton's brows were dragged together into a frown as he hung up. Why had she reacted the way she had when he'd said he thought of going to Dr. Morelle? Almost as if she was scared of him doing just that. The niggling suspicions of the previous night started up in his brain once more. He lit a cigarette, it would help to clear his mind. He went into the little kitchen. The woman who kept his apartment clean had been and gone. No doubt she thought he was sleeping off a night on a bender, he thought grimly. He made himself some strong black coffee. Later he went into the bathroom, washed, shaved and dressed.

As he knotted his tie and stared at his haggard face in the dressing-table mirror, he wondered how long Levaque would stay at the villa. What kind of questions he was asking Stacey. Had he got hold of some new bit of evidence that pointed the finger of suspicion at her or himself? They'd told the blasted man the truth last night. Told him everything. Fenton reassured himself and

tried to feel confident that the detective could have nothing on him. Or on Stacey. Had Levaque found the gun, he wondered, and matched it up with the bullets from Laking's body?

Had there been any mark on the gun that proved it to be Laking's? He glanced at his wrist-watch. It was nearly an hour since Stacey had phoned. He paced about the room. How much longer must he wait? How much more time was he going to have to spend interminably waiting? Yesterday evening, he'd waited for Stacey to get in touch with him. And when she had, it had been too late. And now he was waiting for her again. He supposed he ought to see her before he went to Dr. Morelle, if he decided that was the best move for him to make. Surely Levaque couldn't still be at the villa? He looked out of the window at the sunshine and the blueness of sky and distant sea, shimmering in the golden light of the day. He lit another cigarette.

He went into the kitchen with the idea of burning up a little time making

some more coffee. He didn't really want it, but this waiting frayed your nerves, ate away at your courage.

The telephone started to ring.

21

Stacey Laking had finished telephoning Dyke Fenton just as Sara came in to her room to tell her lunch was ready.

'It's no use,' she said. 'I'm much too upset to eat.'

'I know you're not hungry,' Sara said, 'nor am I, but after that session with Levaque we both need something. Come on down.'

'Dyke's on his way over,' Stacey said.

'He can join us over the eats,' Sara said. 'And we can tell him all about this morning.'

She went out and presently Stacey came downstairs and went into the sitting-room where there was some cold food waiting and some wine. Sara had already started lunch and smiled at Stacey encouragingly. Stacey stood looking through the french windows on to the terrace, which was flooded with sunlight. Outside, the garden was brilliant with

flowers, warmly inviting. It was impossible to believe that last night's tragedy had really happened. She turned to watch Sara pour her out a glass of Sauterne, then put some salad on a plate of cold chicken for her.

'You're behaving marvellously, Sara,' she said. 'I wish I wasn't feeling as scared as I am.'

Sara grinned wryly. 'I am feeling not too cosy myself. But it'll work out, I'm sure. It must. And as soon as the police find who really did do it, what'll we have to worry about then?' Her face clouded as she saw Stacey's expression. 'Oh, I know it's ghastly for you, about Ian, but try not to think about it.' Stacey began to peck at her food and sip some wine. Sara said, 'Has Dyke had any bright ideas?'

'He didn't say so. He must be pretty worried. He's anxious to know what Levaque wanted this morning.'

Sara made an effort to keep her tone light and casual. 'You know quite well the wretched man had to ask you about every little thing, but that doesn't mean he's suspicious of you, nor of Dyke. He asked

me one or two things, too.'

Stacey put down her wine-glass. 'Yes, but the way he pointed out that it seemed unlikely Ian could have been shot by someone who didn't know him and who hadn't actually been to this villa, that makes it look so nasty. Nothing's been stolen, so it couldn't have been a burglar. Don't you see, Sara, it's obvious what conclusion he's come to?'

'I don't see,' Sara said briskly. 'Not if you mean it must be one of us. I just don't see how, because those blood-hounds can't find a clue, it means anything like that. Anyway, Levaque's English goes a little peculiar at times, so he may have said what he didn't mean, or the other way round.'

'He made sense all right to me,' Stacey said. 'It's Dyke and me he's got his eyes on. I know he suspects us of having an affair.' Sara glanced at her as if she didn't think that was so incriminating, but Stacey shook her head hopelessly. 'And by telling him the truth,' she said, 'we've made things worse for ourselves. French police look for a triangle in a case like

this. Levaque thinks he's found one.'

'That's nonsense.' Sara sounded a little impatient. 'He hasn't a scrap of proof and he knows it, and so do you.' She pushed her drink aside and leaned towards Stacey, her expression serious. 'How do we know Ian hadn't made an enemy lately? Here in Monte Carlo, even. It's not impossible. He was in a strange mental state, we all know that now. He could have upset someone, or wronged them. Or it might have been someone in London, who'd come out here in search of revenge.'

'I can't believe anything so melodramatic as that.'

'I wouldn't have believed anything so melodramatic could have happened last night,' Sara said quickly. 'But it did.'

'I wish I knew what was best to do,' Stacey said. 'I'm thinking of Dyke. It's so easy to fall into a trap, say something you think is innocent but which is pounced on because someone sees it in a different way. Dyke is wondering if the only thing to do isn't to put ourselves in Dr. Morelle's hands.'

Sara looked at her thoughtfully. She gave a nod of agreement. 'If you could get him on our side,' she said, 'you'd be all right. Even that French detective seemed a bit in awe of him. But he doesn't look easy to approach.' She took a drink from her glass of wine slowly. 'Only trouble is,' she said slowly, 'that he knows more than the police, and what he knows doesn't look too good for Dyke.'

'The letter, you mean?' Stacey said, her eyes clouded. 'But at least he's held on to it. So far.'

'Only till evening,' Sara said. 'Then he's going to give it to Levaque.'

At that moment they heard footsteps outside and Dyke Fenton came into the room. With a quick pang of concern Stacey saw how grim and tired he looked.

Sara had crossed to him as he stood there, forcing a smile at them. 'You'll have something to eat?'

He shook his head. 'I grabbed a late breakfast,' he said casually. 'I could use a drink. Okay, I'll fix it myself.' And while Sara sat down again he poured himself out a gin-and-tonic. He turned to Stacey.

'How did it go?' he said.

Stacey Laking shrugged hopelessly, then she pushed her chair back from the table, biting her lower lip. Sara was talking.

'I told Stacey she's upsetting herself unnecessarily,' she said. 'I don't believe the police suspect any of us. Just because they haven't a clue they've implied that the murderer must be someone who knew Ian. Or at any rate who knew his way round here.'

Fenton looked from her back to Stacey. He said cheerfully: 'Is that what Levaque was getting at this morning, Stacey?'

She nodded dumbly and he moved to her and took her hand. It was cold, as cold and shaky as it had been last night when he had left her. 'Don't let it worry you,' he said. 'I think Sara's right. These aren't like our own police, they may be trying to trick something out of you if they can. You can't blame Levaque for taking advantage of the situation, if that's how they work here. We're in a spot, you and I, at first sight anyhow. But I don't see he has a shred of evidence against us.

In fact, you and I know he can't have.'

Sara murmured approvingly. 'Just what I told her, Dyke. Scare tactics, that's what Levaque is trying to use.'

Stacey gave them both a wan smile.

'Stacey says you're thinking of going to Dr. Morelle,' Sara said. 'Asking him for help.'

'I think it might be a good plan.' Stacey got up from the table and he lit a cigarette for her. 'What did Levaque say?'

She went across and sat on the window seat, she was twisting her fingers together nervously. 'The same as Sara says. They hadn't been able to find anything that suggested it was someone unknown to Ian. Levaque didn't believe it was a burglar. He thought that whoever it was killed Ian was someone who knew him well, who'd overheard the scene between you and him in the library.'

'That's more or less what I told him last night,' Fenton said.

Sara had taken a cigarette and Dyke turned away from Stacey to give the other a light. Sara took a deep drag at the cigarette. 'Thanks,' she said to Dyke. He

was watching Stacey once more.

'I know,' she was saying, 'but the way he talked this morning made it sound as if he was sceptical of the whole story. He asked a lot of questions about you, how long had I known you, how long had you been with Ian, a whole string of questions.' She gave a sharp laugh. 'You can see what he's after, can't you, Dyke? He's trying to convince himself you and I were — were lovers.'

Dyke grinned briefly. 'I suppose you can't blame a Frenchman for thinking that, it's dead in character. '*Cherchez la femme*,' and all that.' He had lit a cigarette for himself and he said slowly, after a pause: 'That's all we get telling them the true facts. Who said honesty was the best policy?'

It was ironic, he was thinking bitterly. Neither Stacey nor himself had known what they really felt for each other. Neither of them had even realized the attraction existed, until she'd told him about her husband at his apartment yesterday. And Laking was dead then. He glanced at her now. Had he been

presuming? Did she, in fact, feel the same way about him as he knew now he felt about her? Her eyes met his frankly. He would have bet a million on it, he told himself. She looked away, and he caught Sara's glance.

'What else did he say?' he said to Stacey.

'He asked me about the gun,' she said. There was a tremor in her voice. 'I'd never seen one and I told him so. I suppose he didn't believe me. The gendarme who came with him searched around. He started on the garden. He was looking all the time Levaque talked to me, he must have combed it pretty thoroughly. Then he came back and went round the house. But he didn't find anything.' She shivered, despite the summer warmth of the room.

'He didn't find it,' Sara said firmly, 'because the damned thing wasn't here. The murderer took it with him. That's obvious.'

Fenton gave her a brief glance of agreement. The only thing was, he was asking himself, how did the murderer

know where the gun was hidden in the chest outside? He turned back to Stacey. 'Anything else, or did he leave you in peace then?'

'He went soon after that,' she said. 'But Levaque said he might need to come again.'

'Did he mention anything about — about the bullets in Ian's body?'

'He told me about that,' Sara said, as Stacey twisted her head away and fell silent. Dyke looked at Stacey. 'He asked me pretty much the same thing he asked Stacey,' Sara said. 'He said there were three bullets in — ' She broke off with a sidelong look at Stacey, who buried her face in her hands.

'Did he say what calibre?'

'No, he didn't say anything about that.'

'The automatic Ian gave me was fully loaded,' Dyke said. 'Where he got it, God knows. And God knows where it is now.'

'I'd had a look round for it, too,' Sara said. She had moved to Stacey and placed a hand on her shoulders comfortingly. 'But I didn't find it. I didn't expect to.'

Dyke said grimly: 'I'm convinced it was

Ian's gun the murderer used. I wish I knew where the hell it was.'

'It's not here, or it would have been found,' Stacey said. 'If only you hadn't hidden it,' she said bitterly.

'I agree,' Dyke Fenton said. 'I thought I was doing the wise thing. I didn't want the damned gun on me.' His face darkened. As Sara and Stacey watched him, they saw his jaw-muscles tauten as he came to a decision. 'We can't fight this by ourselves,' he said through his teeth. 'We know we're innocent, but the cards are stacked against us. And there are only a few hours before Dr. Morelle hands over that letter to Levaque.'

'Will you go and see him?' Stacey said, and he thought he saw fear showing in her eyes.

He nodded. 'I'll tell him Levaque's been nagging at you. He'll be nagging at me again, too, I shouldn't wonder. And before long.' He went to the door. 'I'll phone him. See if he'll let me go over and talk to him.'

Stacey followed him into the hall and waited while he got through to the Villa

Midnight. A feminine voice answered at the other end. 'Can I speak to Dr. Morelle,' Fenton said.

'I'm afraid he's out, I don't expect him back until this evening. No, I can't tell you where he's to be found. This is Miss Frayle, Dr. Morelle's secretary. Can I ask him to ring you when he comes in?'

'My name's Fenton. Dyke Fenton.' He gave the telephone-number of the Villa des Fleurs and his apartment, explaining that he could be reached at one or the other. 'I want to see Dr. Morelle urgently.'

'I really couldn't be definite about it,' Miss Frayle said, 'but I expect him back before dinner. I'll give him your message at once.'

Fenton hung up and turned to Stacey. His face was grim. Sara had come into the hall and was looking at him hopefully.

'He wasn't there?' Stacey said to him, trying to hide her anxiety in her voice.

'No,' Dyke Fenton said. 'Not till this evening.'

22

Miss Frayle sat at the elegant Italian writing-desk in the library at the Villa Midnight, thoughtfully eyeing the telephone whose receiver she had just replaced. Her gaze wandered to the colonnaded terrace on to which the tall french windows opened and beyond that the garden, filled with what seemed to be every flower under the sun, of every imaginable colour and scent, and beyond that was the magnificent coastline stretched hazily in the afternoon sun away towards Italy.

Fenton. The man broke in on her musings about the luxurious glamour of the scene. The name and that of the Villa des Fleurs rang a bell. Dr. Morelle had mentioned the goings-on at the Villa des Fleurs as being one of the distractions which threatened to interrupt his work. Dyke Fenton. Yes, that was the name. Dr. Morelle had made a brief reference to some strange and unpleasant business in

which he had become involved.

Someone had died at the Villa des Fleurs last night. A publisher, by whom Dyke Fenton was, or had been, employed. And there was the dead man's wife and his secretary. They were all staying in Monte Carlo. It had all sounded a bit peculiar to Miss Frayle, but it was none of her business and she wasn't particularly anxious to allow such happenings to turn this little holiday into another worrying job, of the sort to which she had not been altogether unaccustomed when she'd been with Dr. Morelle in Harley Street.

Meeting Dr. Morelle in the aquarium that morning had been a stroke of good fortune. Of course it was in the hopes of seeing him that she had come to Monte Carlo in the first place, but she had never anticipated staying here, at this sumptuous, simply marvellous villa.

She had moved in full of excited anticipation. The excitement had faded slightly, as she realized the extent of the work Dr. Morelle had intended her to carry out for him. And if he did allow himself to become involved in this

business at the Villa des Fleurs, it looked as though she might easily find herself back to the same old routine, even if it was in different surroundings.

Her gaze wandered over the desk, one quarter of which was covered with layers of notepaper, each sheet covered in familiar meticulous handwriting. Dr. Morelle's notes. And they awaited her attention.

Dr. Morelle had left the villa shortly after lunch informing her that he should be back in the early evening, but there had been something in his expression which made Miss Frayle doubt that he would be back as early as all that.

Before leaving, he had shown Miss Frayle the library and pointed out the beautiful writing-desk, hinting in his sardonic way that if she had nothing better with which to occupy her mind that afternoon he would appreciate her help.

She should have expected it. It was typical of Dr. Morelle. It wouldn't occur to him that it was a lovely afternoon, that she was on holiday, that the rest of the

villa and the beautiful gardens were waiting to be explored.

Miss Frayle got to her feet and moved round the desk. She straightened her spectacles which had slipped a trifle down her nose. Work could wait. She was going to wander round and make the most of the sunshine.

She left the library and went into the vast hall with its rose-coloured walls, and she went up the wide staircase, marvelling at the hand-carved woodwork. She reached the gallery and went to her bedroom. She really couldn't get used to it, and she stood inside the door staring wide-eyed at the wonderful room. It was a dream bedroom, fit for a princess. The décor was a delicate rose-pink and the divan bed as sumptuously soft as the silken eiderdown that covered the bed-spread. There were filmy curtains and the ceiling was carved, small pale pink cherubs smiled down at her. A built-in wash-basin was tucked away in a small alcove, its front covered with a frilled curtain which matched the other soft fabrics of the room.

With a happy sigh Miss Frayle began to change her clothes. She took off the business-like skirt and blouse, washed, made-up her face delicately, then chose a cool, soft apple-green dress from the small collection she had hung in the wardrobe. Then she stepped through the french window on to the spacious balcony.

It was very hot. The birds sang lazily, quietly. The view across the garden to the sea shimmered in a heat-haze as the sun poured down from a cloudless blue sky. The town was taking its siesta, waiting for the shadows of evening to bring back its energy. Two or three small yachts moved slowly on the sea, a mile or so from the shore, but there was only a faint breeze which stirred the strands of Miss Frayle's hair. It came off the land and there was no coolness in it.

The garden tumbled below in scented colour ablaze with purples and gold, scarlet and rich blue. The orange-trees and tangerine-trees, the rubber-trees and the palms spread their shadows over the close-cropped lawn like dark umbrellas.

She turned and went back into the room and down the stairs.

Miss Frayle wandered about the garden. She met no one and among the trees and flowers behind the villa she could imagine herself miles from anywhere. She found the ornamental lake with its gold and silver fish darting like flashes of sunlight through the limpid water. On the far side the great leaves of water lilies swam lazily on the surface and from somewhere beyond came the croak of a frog. It was very still and peaceful by the pool and the only other visitor was a small lizard that lay sleeping in the sun on a flat slab of rock which formed one side of the lake. When Miss Frayle approached for a closer inspection it woke suddenly and slid swiftly away, to be lost in a shadowy niche of the rocks.

Miss Frayle sat on a white-painted seat and abandoned herself to a wonderful waking dream in which she was the Comtesse, this was her villa, and Dr. Morelle was staying with her.

At last she made her way back to the white-walled villa through the sunken

garden. When she reached the terrace the house-keeper appeared and asked in awkward English if Miss Frayle would like to take tea on the terrace? Miss Frayle said she would.

For the next half hour she sat alone at one of the wicker tables sipping from expensive china and eating the newly-baked French scones which the house-keeper had brought out to her.

Her thoughts turned somewhat wistfully again to the Comtesse. What sort of a person was she? Miss Frayle had heard Dr. Morelle speak of her in admiring tones. Too admiring to please Miss Frayle. She was obviously loaded. The Villa Midnight was evidence enough of that, and she was now spending some months in America.

Miss Frayle was suddenly racked with guilt. Here she was wallowing in all this luxury and disliking the one to whom it all belonged heartily at the same time. She knew it was absurd to feel this faint twinge of jealousy where Dr. Morelle was concerned, but she couldn't shake it off.

The house-keeper came back to collect

the tea-things. When she had filled the tray she hovered respectfully. She was a dumpy, rather swarthy woman, very neat in appearance and with snapping, black eyes. Privately, Miss Frayle thought her eyes a bit too close together and wondered if the woman was honest, and then dismissed the suspicion. After all, it wasn't her silver, anyway. It was obvious she wanted to ask something, and Miss Frayle asked her what it was.

'Do you know, mademoiselle, how long it will be before Dr. Morelle returns?'

'I'm afraid I've no idea,' Miss Frayle said. 'I hope it will be before dinner. Why?'

The woman stumbled over her words. 'It is just that he agreed to let my husband and me go early this evening,' she said, 'so that we might visit our god-child, who is celebrating his saint's day to-day. We are expected and we should not like to cause any disappointment, you understand?'

Miss Frayle nodded. 'Of course. If Dr. Morelle knows about it, you must go.

Please tell your husband it is quite all right.' The woman's husband worked in the garden at the Villa Midnight and attended to the various odd jobs around the place. The couple's name was Boillot.

With suitable protestations of gratitude the woman went off, and a few minutes later Miss Frayle saw the two of them going down the drive towards the wrought-iron gates. Picking up an illustrated magazine that lay nearby Miss Frayle leaned back in her chair and began idly turning the glossy pages. Dusk would soon be falling, but the air was still warm, even close. She felt a little drowsy. It would be pleasant to close her eyes and day-dream about Dr. Morelle. This evening she would be alone with him. They would dine together. But before they went in to dinner there would be cocktails on the terrace — perhaps, if he was late, in the moonlight.

Miss Frayle woke suddenly.

For a second she wondered where she was, then she jumped up, a little shocked to find she had fallen asleep, and for so long. It was becoming dark. The stars

were beginning to pierce the velvety sky. The house lay silent behind her. She was suddenly conscious of the silence.

How different everything looked. The garden was no longer friendly and inviting, she thought. Everywhere there were shadows, and the dark blur of the trees seemed to reach to the terrace to hide her in blackness. Miss Frayle went quickly inside and switched the lights on. She closed the french windows and the doors.

It was then that she realized for the first time that she was alone in the villa.

She thought of the other villa, the Villa des Fleurs, and for no reason she could think of, her throat felt suddenly dry. A drink, she thought. A glass of light wine, or a little gin-and-tonic. It was stupid to get panicky just because she was alone in this marvellous place. She found the drinks in the studio, in a lovely Louis XV cabinet. There were wines, but after a moment's hesitation she chose some gin. She poured a measure, added tonic-water and ice, drank it, choked, and felt better.

It was childish, she told herself yet

again, to be afraid of the dark, to be frightened in such lovely surroundings. Besides, Dr. Morelle would surely be back soon. Suddenly she remembered she had done none of the work he had left her. The notes were still waiting on the writing-desk in the library.

She made her way there, saw that the french windows leading to the terrace were closed, and then she sat at the desk and began to sift out the notes. She half-wished Dr. Morelle would not come for a while so that she would have some work to show him when he did arrive. The notes needed to be sorted out into chronological order, then they could be typed out. Dr. Morelle hadn't mentioned a typewriter and she wondered if there was one in the villa. She wouldn't put it past him if he asked her why she hadn't brought her own typewriter with her. She giggled a little to herself, the gin-and-tonic was going to her head, she told herself, and smiled some more.

She concentrated, staring at Dr. Morelle's handwriting. By keeping her mind on the

task she would forget she was alone in the villa.

But she could not forget. The feeling of uneasiness which had caught at her heart when she had awoken on the terrace was still there. And once again she found her thoughts turning to the Villa des Fleurs.

23

Dyke Fenton stayed on with Stacey and Sara at the Villa des Fleurs until late afternoon. They discussed the one subject that concerned them all, discussed it until it was exhausted, and then started all over again.

Fenton grew sick of talking, talking about the ghastly night the three of them had endured. It was getting them nowhere. There was nothing to be done until he saw Dr. Morelle, and he couldn't do that until the evening. Flinging questions at each other was only another way of rubbing salt into their raw nerves. And all the time, every moment he looked at Stacey, heard her voice, watched the nervous movements of her sun-tanned hands, there hovered at the back of his mind the nagging doubt and suspicion that she knew more than she pretended. When Sara said she was going to see about rustling up some tea, to cheer

themselves up a bit, he took the opportunity to leave.

Before he went he told them both not to worry. He promised to get in touch with Stacey again before he contacted Dr. Morelle. Then he went out of the coolness of the villa into the blue and glitter, the heat of the afternoon.

Dyke Fenton's mind was anxious, his body irritated by the heat which stuck his shirt to his back as he found himself walking with nervously unnecessary speed. The golden serenity of the afternoon that would soon be closing on the day seemed a mockery. He wanted to hide himself away, draw a blanket of darkness over himself and sleep, and when he woke, find all this horror was nothing more than a nightmare that had passed with his waking.

He half expected to find Levaque awaiting him at his apartment. He let himself in and went in to the sitting-room and began pouring himself a drink. He realized that he was experiencing a kind of let-down at the failure of Levaque to put in an appearance. He'd chatted

enough to Sara and Stacey, why had the detective left him out of it? After all, wasn't he the number one suspect?

He mooched into the bathroom and showered, put on fresh clothes and returned to the sitting-room. He lit a cigarette and went across to the window, staring unseeingly out. He decided that Levaque was playing it the subtle way, at least it was meant to be subtle. He was letting him sweat on the top line, leaving him to make a false move that would give himself away to the detective. But there wasn't a false move he could make.

He thought about giving Dr. Morelle a ring, but held back. After all if he'd returned to the Villa Midnight, that secretary of his would have given him the message and Dr. Morelle would have called him back.

Then it occurred to him that Levaque may have unwittingly played into his hands by leaving him alone. Suppose Levaque had come to see him, he'd have felt cornered. He didn't want to answer any more questions until he'd seen Dr. Morelle, and if Levaque had chatted away

to him in that deceptively casual way of his, it might have been too late to call in Dr. Morelle anyway.

He looked down into the road, he wondered if Levaque had put a man on to tail him, but he could see no one hanging about. On an impulse he went out of the apartment and ran down to the road. He passed a nursemaid pushing an expensive-looking perambulator, and a tall, thin man with a Pekinese dog some distance beyond her. Fenton gave them a suspicious glance as he passed quickly, he knew he was nerving himself to call at the Villa Midnight and wait there for Dr. Morelle, if he hadn't yet returned.

Evening was drifting in from the sea, the sky was beginning to mass into brilliant fantastic colours. Now and again the sea was visible from deep tree-lined roads, growing purple and shimmering in the gathering dusk.

Dyke Fenton saw none of the strange beauty, the almost tropical fascination of the scene. His mind was pushing round the treadmill of conjecture and suspicion. Stacey and Laking, the woman he knew

now he loved and her husband. Then his thoughts grappled with Levaque. There was little doubt which way Levaque's mind was working. *Cherchez la femme*, Fenton thought savagely. And then look for the lover. The lover of the wife of the man who was dead. It was as easy as that for a French policeman. *Crime passionelle*, and all the rest of it.

The gun? Levaque would accuse him of throwing it in the sea, anywhere. That, and the letter Dr. Morelle held, could clinch his guilt, a letter written by a madman, cunningly contrived to finish him. And who could prove Laking had been insane? Could Dr. Morelle? Even he hadn't had a chance of meeting Laking before he died. Could Dr. Morelle, on the evidence say that Laking was a raving, vindictive madman?

Fenton knew now more than ever, that he must see Dr. Morelle, put all his cards on the table. He realized suddenly that night had closed in and he had walked so far he was not certain where he was. He stopped and looked round him. He was on the crest of a hill. He could see the

glitter of Monte Carlo spread out below him. He was some way beyond the fringe of the town. Which was the quickest way back? He had promised to telephone Stacey before he got in touch with Dr. Morelle.

He kept on walking. The trees threw dark shadows before him but the stars were very bright and the road wound downwards and then it levelled out and he saw a well-kept hedge on one side of the road. It looked like the boundary hedge of a villa and a few yards further on he came to a pair of wrought-iron gates. He crossed over and stood at the entrance to a drive.

There was an ornate name plate on the gates but a tall rubber-tree threw its shadow over the entrance and he couldn't read the name. He flicked his lighter into flame and saw that it was the Villa Midnight.

Dyke Fenton shivered in the night air. He made out the faint outline of the villa, white and ghostly in the starlight. He saw that a light burned in one of the tall windows which looked out on a colon-naded terrace. The secretary had told him

she had expected Dr. Morelle back by dinner at the latest. Surely it was past that time now? The light might mean that Dr. Morelle had returned. He might have been trying to phone him at his apartment or the Villa des Fleurs. And he'd been chasing his tail round Monte Carlo like an hysterical girl. He tightened his mouth in a bitter, rueful line. He glanced at his wrist-watch and thumbed his cigarette-lighter again to make out the time. It was approaching eight o'clock. He must have been walking a hell of a lot longer than he'd realized. Time seemed to have lost all sense to him these past twenty-four hours. And he should have phoned Stacey before he spoke to Dr. Morelle. But there was no real reason why he should, he could phone her afterwards, when he'd some news to tell her.

Fate had led him here, he thought grimly. For the first time that evening his depression lifted, he felt calm and confident. He pushed open the iron gate and went towards the villa, looming up at him pale and quiet, almost secretive. Even

in his excitement he noticed how well-kept the extensive gardens were. Shadows from the trees and palms lay across the lawns and the flower beds. The palms rustled eerily, as if he had disturbed them from their sleep as he passed. He could make out the terrace along one side of the house and the balconies at the first floor windows.

Taking a deep breath he went up the steps of the portico. He stood at the front-door beyond which was the darkness of the hall. He pressed the bell and heard the chiming of an elaborate electric bell inside the hall. He waited for a light to come on.

Now beyond the glazed door which was closed against him he thought he could make out a faint glow of light that must be burning somewhere beyond the hall perhaps, or the top of the stairs.

No one answered his ring. Frowning, and a faint shiver of some unknown uneasiness passing down the nape of his neck, he was about to press the bell again. Then he heard footsteps along the hall. A shadowy figure loomed up vaguely

beyond the glass of the door. The door slowly opened, but it was too dark for Fenton to make out who the figure was, half hidden there. He imagined it to be a servant, or perhaps the secretary, the one who'd called herself Miss Frayle.

'I wonder if I could speak to Dr. Morelle?' he said. 'It is most urgent that I should see him.' As the figure didn't answer him, he assumed it wasn't Miss Frayle, who would have realized who he was. 'He'll understand,' he said, 'if you say it's Mr. Fenton.'

The door opened wider but the shadowy figure still didn't answer. Fenton thought maybe she was French and couldn't speak English. But she was inviting him in.

He stepped over the threshold.

It was a woman anyway, he realized by the rustle of her dress as she remained for a second partly behind the door. Fenton glanced along the hall. He was right about the light, it was at the top of the wide staircase. He was wondering irritably why the hall light had not been switched on when there came a sudden

movement at his shoulder.

He thought the woman was closing the door. Then a terrific blow struck him on the side of his head, and the hall and the light suddenly spun round him. The shadows closed in on him and enfolded him in inky blackness.

As he sank into the darkness that came up at him from the floor, he was aware of a faint familiar scent.

24

The Villa des Fleurs looked solid and welcoming as Stacey Laking opened the gate and went quickly along the path towards the front door. She was anxious to get back without Sara knowing that she had been out. If she told Sara that she had gone out for a walk because she wanted to be alone to think, she might not believe her. She could see Sara's room on the first floor. A light was burning. Downstairs the rooms were in darkness. It was not yet eight-thirty, but Stacey guessed that Sara had gone upstairs, she must feel pretty worn-out herself and she was trying to get an early night. Stacey sighed. When would she feel like sleep again?

As she neared the steps to the doorway she thought she saw a movement in the garden. Instantly she thought of Levaque. Or was her nervousness and the shadows playing tricks on her? When she paused to

stare into the shadows she could see there was no one there. The orange trees threw deep pools of blackness over the steps and beyond them past the villa the darkness seemed to be full of movement. But there was no one there. She was alone in the garden.

Stacey stood at the foot of the steps and glanced along the white terrace, her thoughts running round her head as if caught in a mill-race.

Then again a sudden movement, this time in the shadows at the end of the terrace caught her eye. She was sure this time someone was there, so that she stopped where she was. Was that Levaque or one of his men lurking there, watching her? She thought she could make out a shape. The shadow seemed to sway a little. Then she saw that all the shadows were swaying. It was the night breeze off the sea.

Stacey told herself to stop acting like a nervous child. She walked quickly up the steps and into the hall, quietly closing the door behind her, and locking it. The servant had gone after she had served an

early cold supper, which Stacey and Sara had eaten without much enthusiasm on Stacey's part, though the other had urged her typically that she must eat, that she must relax on everything. Stacey had drunk some wine, and then plenty of black coffee.

She went into the sitting-room and she switched on the light and stood listening. Was that Sara in the hall? What was she doing there, had she been awaiting her return? Had she heard her slip out of the villa? For a dreadful moment she thought she would completely lose control, it was all she could do not to scream out. She bit her lower lip and tensed herself. And then she relaxed a little. She went out into the hall.

Sara wasn't there. The hall was as empty as it had been when she had come in, as empty as she knew now the garden had been. Gradually, as she went back to the brightly-lit room, she felt her fears of the darkness, the shadows, recede like a tide, leaving her nerves still raw and exposed. She went to the window and drew the curtains, shutting out the night.

As she smoked a cigarette, Stacey saw that her fingers were trembling. There was no escape, she thought. She had hurried from the Villa des Fleurs, driven by an irresistible urge.

She shivered, although the air in the room was warm. She swung round as Sara stood in the doorway. She was wearing a dressing-gown of a masculine cut. She came into the room. 'I thought I heard someone down here,' she said with a smile. 'I thought it might be Dyke, I'd no idea it was you.'

'I came downstairs and tried to think,' Stacey said. 'I suppose I've been waiting for Dyke to phone. He said he would, before he tried to see Dr. Morelle.'

'Yes, I know,' Sara said, 'he must have forgotten and gone to the Villa Midnight, perhaps he's still there.'

Stacey looked at her. 'But why should he have forgotten to phone?' She pushed a hand through her hair and turned away as if the answer to her question didn't matter.

'Poor Stacey,' Sara said softly. 'It's rotten for you. If I'd known you were

down here I'd have come down myself. I thought I'd do some work, so I started wading through that manuscript that Dyke brought over, for — for poor Ian to read.' She paused and then said lightly: 'It's got something. I think it's got something.'

Stacey nodded as if she wanted to hear more, she was glad that Sara wasn't going to question her, ask her if she'd been out. How could she explain that to her? How could she tell her what impulses of desperation had impelled her? Sara went on about the manuscript, apparently glad that Stacey was showing some interest in it. Stacey realized that Sara was herself grateful to talk about something that had nothing to do with the horror of last night.

'You didn't hear the phone?' Stacey said presently. 'While I was out — in the garden?'

'No. I was upstairs in my room, but I'd have heard. I wasn't so engrossed in the manuscript as all that.' She started talking about the manuscript again, enthusing.

Stacey stubbed her cigarette out

nervously. She didn't want to hear any more. She wished the other would stop talking.

'He promised to get in touch with me first,' she said. 'I can't make it out.'

Sara looked at her, and it seemed to be an effort for her to bring her mind back to Stacey's anxiety for Dyke. 'Maybe you'd better ring him, see if he's at the apartment.'

Stacey said she would, she spoke quickly, it was as if she couldn't understand why she hadn't thought of doing it before. They went out into the hall and Stacey got through to the number. She held the receiver out to Sara, they both listened to the monotonous ringing at the other end. Stacey held it for a long time, then she slowly replaced the receiver. 'He can't be there,' she said slowly.

'He must have gone to see Dr. Morelle then,' Sara said. 'Why don't you ring him there?'

'I don't know the number,' Stacey said. 'And anyway, perhaps it'd be better if I didn't phone him there.' Her voice trailed

off and Sara gave a little shrug.

Stacey Laking suddenly put up her hands and covered her eyes. 'This waiting. What are we going to do, Sara?'

Sara said quietly: 'We can't do anything, Stacey. Dyke will turn up before long, or he'll phone you. That's for sure. Come on up to your room. I know you won't sleep but at least you ought to lie down and rest. You'll crack up if you go on like this.'

Wearily Stacey followed Sara up the stairs. At the door of her room she paused, forced a smile and said, 'I'll be all right, Sara. I'll just lie down. You'll be in your room, won't you?'

'Call me if you want anything. Good night, Stacey, and try to take it easy.'

Stacey murmured gratefully and went into her room, closing the door behind her.

Sara watched her, eyes narrowed and the questions simmering in her mind. After a few moments she turned and went back to her own room.

25

Dyke Fenton was conscious of the pain knifing through one side of his head. He struggled to open his eyes. It took some time and even when they were open he found he couldn't focus. Lights and shadows danced about in front of him. Slowly everything settled into pattern.

He was lying on the tessellated marble hall-floor. He felt sick and his head was throbbing. Gingerly he put up his hand and felt the bump just under his hair. It was damned painful, but there was no blood. He got to his feet slowly, and dizzily stared round.

Things were coming back to him. He was in the hall of Dr. Morelle's villa. The Villa Midnight. He had rung the bell and someone, he had realized it was a woman, had opened the door. She had held it open, inviting him in. She had not spoken. He hadn't seen her clearly because she was half-hidden behind the

door. He had stepped into the hall and then it had happened.

He groaned. Yes, he'd taken a nasty smack over the head. But why? Who the devil would want to knock him out? And in Dr. Morelle's villa. It just didn't make sense.

Dyke Fenton turned to the front door. Behind him was the glow from a light upstairs. The house was silent. Not a squeak anywhere. The glazed door before him was closed. His hand shifted along the wall for the electric light switch. His fingers fumbled, found it. The hall was flooded with light that dazzled his eyes, making him blink painfully.

It was a spacious hall with luxurious rugs spread over the floor. He had fallen upon one, which had been luck for him, he reflected grimly, he might have caught his head on the marble and concussed himself. There was a cactus plant in a handsome pot near the window, a low cream wrought-iron table with a large bowl of roses and a telephone on it, a rich carpet on the cream stair-case. And no one to appreciate it but himself. The

house stayed silent save for the ticking of a clock somewhere.

He glanced at his watch. It hadn't been damaged apparently in his fall, it was still ticking away quietly. It said the time was coming up for ten-fifty. He found himself vaguely trying to work out what that was in Continental time, but gave up, as his head started to throb, and he called out Dr. Morelle's name. No one answered and the silence washed back over him like an invisible sea.

How long had he been unconscious? He had shown up at the Villa Midnight around eight, or maybe later, he couldn't be sure of the exact time. Where was his assailant? The woman who'd hit hard enough to lay him out cold for about four hours. He was certain she was not in the house. Maybe she'd been on the point of leaving when he rang the bell. Fenton flung open the glazed door and went out on the steps. He moved across the portico and stared out over the garden, which lay bathed in the soft starlight.

Nothing stirred. The garden appeared deserted. He looked across the lawn to

the shadows cast by the trees. The air struck him quite cool and refreshing. He decided that his head was clearing slowly, though the pain still hung around there. He stood looking about him for a time and then his attention was drawn to the distant slopes of the Alpes Maritimes pushing up against the stars that winked at him from everywhere in the purplish dome overhead.

He had left the door open, and light from the hall splashed across the portico and threw his long shadow zig-zagging down the steps. He saw that the light was still on in the french windows opening on to the terrace at the side of the house, the light he had seen from the gate when he approached.

He suddenly remembered Dr. Morelle's secretary. The house looked deserted, but was it? If it seemed apparent that Dr. Morelle had still not returned, what about the woman who'd answered the phone to him, Miss Frayle she called herself? When she'd spoken to him she hadn't implied that she was going to be out that evening.

He turned back quickly to the front

door. The violent movement made his head throb, but he ignored the pain. Once inside the hall he closed the door. He called out for Dr. Morelle once more, he made it louder this time, he was feeling better, but there was no sound in reply.

He opened the door to his left and switched on the light. This must be a sort of studio, he thought, eyeing the elegant furniture, the white rugs. The air was fragrant with grasse roses and jasmin. He glanced up at the crystal lights which threw a diffused glow on to the painted ceiling.

He went back to the hall and opened doors, the rooms of which were completely dark, until he opened the door to a room which was not dark, but where a light burned, a soft light over the writing-desk. This appeared empty too.

Dyke Fenton stared around the library where bookshelves lined one whole side of the room. The curtains had been drawn across the window. They were the same colour as the thick, soft carpet under his feet. The fireplace was masked by an Italian decorated screen.

His gaze fixed itself on the wide writing-desk. The lamp glowed over the papers strewn all over the desk. It was then that he saw the figure slumped down in the chair behind the desk, almost hidden from view from where he was standing. As he crossed the room, he saw that it was a slim, fair-haired girl whose horn-rimmed spectacles had slipped down her nose.

He went round the desk and lifted the shade of the lamp so that the naked light spilled over her.

She was out cold, as cold as he'd been. A discoloration of the skin just above her temple showed what had happened. She had been hit with something. The same object that had been used on him? The same attacker? There was no doubt of it, he told himself. He stared down at her and concluded that this must be Miss Frayle, secretary to Dr. Morelle.

She was breathing normally, a little noisily but her respiration was all right. He guessed she must have been struck down before he got to the villa.

Who had done it, he asked himself, was it Laking's murderer? The question

flamed in his mind. But if so, why come here?

Dyke Fenton felt gripped in a chill, a chill as icy as death. He began shaking visibly as there came to him then the sudden recollection of the scent in his nostrils, the scent that had reached him as he had fallen into the black pit of unconsciousness out there in the hall.

He felt sick to the stomach with horror. He knew now whose perfume it was.

26

Dyke Fenton stared down at the slumped figure of Miss Frayle. It was at once apparent to him that the same person had done it, whoever it was who had knocked him out. And who had shot Laking in the back? It didn't necessarily add up to that, and yet his mind leapt to that probability.

He remembered the suspicion that had wriggled into his thoughts before, and which he had resolutely tried to thrust away. But now there was this scent that lingered in his nostrils, the scent of which he had been aware, in that interminable second before he had lost consciousness. It was one thing a man never forgot, the scent worn by the woman he loved.

But why would Stacey have wanted to attack him? Why attack Miss Frayle? There seemed to be only one answer to it. A fearfully obvious answer. If Stacey was responsible she had acted that way to ensure her presence at the Villa Midnight

was not known. But why had she come here? He stared at the untidy desk. There was something here he failed completely to understand. A thought occurred to him that perhaps she had visited Dr. Morelle to plead for the letter her husband had written to him in his insane jealousy, to ask him to destroy it, perhaps. Only she had found that Dr. Morelle had not yet returned. So she had talked to Miss Frayle, asked her for the incriminating letter. Supposing, as would be most likely, Miss Frayle had refused to hand it over? And then Stacey had panicked, knocked Miss Frayle unconscious and grabbed the letter. That could be it, he told himself. That added up.

But even if that was what had happened, and he found it incredible that Stacey Laking could have been responsible for such a desperate action, it didn't explain the attack on himself. Why would she strike at him? Surely if she'd come to get the letter on his behalf, she would not have minded his unexpected arrival on the scene, she would have welcomed him and informed him of what she had

achieved, the reason for her own presence there. It just didn't make sense. Unless Stacey had something to hide, something which she had been so terrified of his finding out that she had attacked him in the darkness and knocked him unconscious.

Fenton realized sickeningly that he was doubting Stacey as he had done before. It was despicable, it was madness to allow a scrap of circumstantial evidence in the form of a hint of some scent to channel his suspicions against her, to wonder if she had been involved in her own husband's brutal murder. This was the way Levaque might be thinking, this was the line the detective, determined to produce someone to answer for the crime, would be expected to pursue.

He eyed the papers on the desk, littered with documents. Notes apparently concerned with Dr. Morelle's work, it was erudite stuff, way over his head. He wrenched a drawer out which stood half-open to his gaze, and he observed that it had been disturbed already.

Someone had searched it hurriedly, as they had searched everywhere on the writing-desk, and he saw that the contents of the other drawers had been pushed around and hastily slammed shut. Making a desperate attempt to find that damned letter, that seemed clear enough. But had the searcher found it, or had Dr. Morelle perhaps been carrying the letter on him?

With an effort Dyke Fenton thrust aside the queries that seared his mind. There was this secretary to think about. He held her wrist and to his relief the pulse was strong and regular. She gave a little moan and he straightened up and stood looking at her slumped form, perplexity drawing his brows together. It struck him finally that the moment she regained consciousness she'd immediately suppose it was he who'd attacked her. She'd be dazed, confused, but she'd be bound to accuse him. There was no one to support his story, that he had called to see Dr. Morelle, that he found himself drawn, as it were, to the Villa Midnight, and he too had been

attacked as he stepped inside the door. How was he going to explain all this to her?

All the same he couldn't leave her like that, he had to take a chance and help her, and he went quickly out of the library to fetch some iced water from the studio. He recalled seeing some ice-cubes and a carafe among the bottles and decanters and glasses on the drinks table. As he started to splash some water into a glass he heard the scrape of shoes on the steps outside.

Dyke Fenton stood perfectly still, holding his breath. Who could it be? Dr. Morelle, or the servants returning, no doubt. Unless it was the unseen assailant coming back for some dark purpose. Or Levaque?

He knew he mustn't be found in the house. He could slip out through the french windows across the room. But he wanted to see who it was, for one thing he wanted to be sure the secretary was found and taken care of. If it was her attacker in fact at the door, he couldn't leave the unconscious young woman to the intruder's mercy.

Yet, and a chill pierced his heart, if it turned out to be not the assailant, nor Dr. Morelle, but that blue-chinned detective, he was done for. He would never be able to talk his way out of this situation. Panic overwhelmed him, as he drew the curtain aside in an effort to see who it was there. But the portico masked the front door and he couldn't make out anyone in the darkness.

Fenton's throat was dry, he knew he had to do it, he had to get away. He felt convinced it was Levaque and panic raged more violently within him. Knowing himself for a wretched coward he edged back the latch of the french window and eased it open as silently as he could. The light in the room threw his shadow momentarily across the terrace as he slipped past the curtain. As he went swiftly on tip-toe along the terrace towards the gate to the road, he knew what he must do. As soon as he got back to his apartment he would telephone the Villa Midnight on some pretext and assure himself that, if Dr. Morelle wasn't there, it was Levaque's arrival which had

disturbed him, and that Miss Frayle was at any rate in good hands.

It was pretty feeble, he told himself miserably, but it was all he dare do. Reaching the end of the terrace he stood listening for a moment, mopping his sweat-beaded and still aching brow with his handkerchief. All was quiet behind him, there was no sound from the villa. He moved out of the shadows, made a dash for it across the garden and gained the darkness of some palms.

At last he made the iron gate and stood in the road, staring back at the villa. Lights were burning in the hall and the library. And he saw light shaft through the half-open french windows of the studio, cutting a pale wedge across the terrace, white in the gloom. He wondered if it was Dr. Morelle who'd arrived. Fervently, he hoped so. He tried to believe that there was no earthly reason why it should be the secretary's and his assailant who had come back. It was the last place to which they would return.

He headed for the Villa des Fleurs. His mind was racing again round the woman

in the darkness, the scent she had worn and all the agonizing suspicions seethed in his brain once more. He had to talk to her, find out the truth. He began looking for a telephone-box. In his desperation, he forgot the inert figure he had left behind him, in the library. It was Stacey he must speak to.

Dyke Fenton found a call-box a couple of hundred yards along the road. The number rang for a long time, then someone picked up the receiver and he heard Stacey's voice.

'Dyke here,' he said. His voice sounded harsh, charged with doubt and anxiety. 'You in bed, Stacey?'

'Dyke,' she said, 'oh, Dyke. Thank God you've telephoned. I've been thinking all sorts of things have happened to you.'

'I hope I didn't wake you,' he said.

'I couldn't sleep,' she said. 'I told you, I've been so worried about you.'

'Poor Stacey,' he said. But his tone was still hard. 'Have you been out this evening, Stacey?'

'I went out earlier, for a walk,' she said.

She sounded surprised. 'My nerves were all jangled.'

'Anywhere particular?' he said, keeping his voice level.

'No, nowhere particular.'

'You didn't call at the Villa Midnight?' He forced a lightness into his question. 'Did you, Stacey?'

'Oh, Dr. Morelle? No, why should I? I thought you were going there.' Her voice sounded brittle with anxiety. 'Dyke, what is all this? You sound strange.'

'I've got to talk to you,' he said. 'I'm coming round. There's one hell of a lot to tell you.'

She was trying to say something to him, but he rang off brutally, pushed his way out of the telephone-kiosk. Stacey had admitted she'd been out for a walk, though she denied having been at the Villa Midnight. Was she telling the truth? What about that scent in the shadows? Her scent, the stuff she always wore.

Dyke Fenton knew he would have no peace until he'd got the truth out of her. And it had to be soon, it had to be now.

27

Dr. Morelle bent his hooded gaze upon the two men in the room at the Hotel Hugo. The french windows opened on to a narrow balcony which overlooked the Casino and the Sporting Club; and not far distant was the Musée Oceanique, where only that morning Dr. Morelle had encountered Miss Frayle; and beyond that the harbour, its yachts like tall ghosts reflected in the dark waters, the stars above seeming to dance gently in the ripples made upon the surface by the lap-lap against the vessels' sides. 'The criminologist's logic is founded upon a major premise from which he reaches his conclusion,' Dr. Morelle was saying. He made a movement with his Le Sphinx in the direction of Levaque, who was listening intently.

'It so happens,' Dr. Morelle said, 'that I am even now engaged in a reassessment of Theodor Reik, of whose enviable

reputation in his field I need not remind you.'

'Ah, a great man,' the detective said, with a respectful nod of his dark head, and the other man muttered in agreement over the short briar pipe stuck between his teeth.

'He forms a large portion of the study of this aspect of crime-detection upon which I am working, which task brought me to Monte Carlo with the object of pursuing it undisturbed by external events.'

Dr. Morelle permitted himself a faint wry smile as the two other men muttered commiseratingly. Levaque took up his glass which sparkled with the Vin Rose from the bottle which stood on the low table before him. He sipped the wine appreciatively, and Dr. Morelle took a drink from his own glass before he went on talking.

'Whereas the analyst must arrive at the identical truth by somewhat different means, means which have little to do with conscious logic, the criminologist relies on his knowledge of the material event

and the ultimate discovery of an unknown person who is the guilty one. The analyst sets out to ascertain the psychological processes and in the elucidation of a crime by psychological means everything except analytical insight is unessential. While to you, of course,' and the Le Sphinx flickered again towards Levaque, 'such insight is unimportant.'

'I am merely a police detective,' the other said with a suitably self-deprecatory smile lighting up his dark-jawed face.

'And an excellent investigator, too,' Dr. Morelle said, 'if I may say so.'

'I could not wish for anyone whom I would rather hear say so,' Levaque said, with a little bow towards the gaunt, saturnine figure who sat opposite him.

'In both your case, and mine,' Dr. Morelle said, 'there are signs, clues, to be observed and interpreted. The difference lies in the type of clue which strikes you as vital, and which appeals to my sense of importance. To you, my dear Levaque, it is the objective sign, some form of inorganic matter, such as a finger-print, a bloodstain, a few particles of dust in the

turn-up of a pair of trousers. These are what tell you tales. But I, while I pay due regard to such items as I come across them, I reach my conclusions through my obversation of the manner in which the persons concerned are behaving, their reactions.'

'But how about if you don't know which persons are the suspects?' the thick-set man with the pipe said.

'Naturally,' Dr. Morelle said, 'one adapts one's methods to the individual circumstances. In this case, however, we are reasonably safe in assuming that this man Laking was murdered by someone with whom he was more or less well acquainted. Our friend here has advised us that his investigations to-day have resulted in his being able to narrow down the number of people who were near or at the scene of the crime at the time it was committed to three only.'

'That is precisely the case,' the detective said, with an air of confident finality.

The sturdy man who had the appearance of a man who spent his time

out-of-doors and who might have been a successful gardener, inclined his head. Dr. Morelle said: 'And so while for me the finger-print may be of only partial interest, I might be fully alert while observing how the individual, Fenton, for example, handled his cigarette-case, shall we say, when he was giving me his account of last night's event.'

Both the others shot quick looks at him. Levaque fell into the trap and said: 'You have already decided that he is our man?'

Dr. Morelle shook his head, a frosty smile touching the corners of his strongly sculptured mouth. 'I made the point that I was quoting him as an example when considering the difference between the way you work and my own methods.' He regarded his cigarette for a moment before he continued. 'I referred to the eminent psychologist and criminologist, Reik,' he said. 'And you may recall that he made an analysis of the Barckhausen affair.'

The other two nodded, and Dr. Morelle recapitulated the strange circumstances which had surrounded the death

of a German consul-general named Von Barckhausen who was found shot dead one warm July evening in 1931, in the study of his home on the outskirts of Berlin. No one suspected that this man was in fact financially ruined; and since everything about his death seemed to point to his having been murdered by a burglar, it was not until it was disclosed that he had left some two hundred thousand marks to his family, which legacy would have been invalid in the event of his committing suicide, that the investigating police considered the possibility of Von Barckhausen having taken his own life.

Dr. Morelle related how subsequent inquiries and the emergence of other clues revealed that, in fact, it was a case of suicide, cunningly rigged to give the impression that it was murder. Dr. Morelle concluded with the observation which brought a gurgling noise from the fresh-complexioned man's pipe, and a sharp exclamation from Levaque: 'No doubt you had observed as I did that well-thumbed volume of which Theodor

Reik is the author, and which contains an account of the Barckhausen case?'

'*Dieu*,' Levaque said, with almost a snarl in his tone which was suddenly no longer casual, 'I did in fact notice it on the writing-desk. It was obscured by the manuscript which the man Fenton said he had brought for Laking to read.'

'Precisely,' Dr. Morelle said.

'But I did not recall its contents.'

'I might not have done myself,' Dr. Morelle said, assuming an air of modesty, 'but that as I mentioned, I am engaged on work to which I owe a not inconsiderable debt to Reik.'

'And that is why you telephoned Sir Trevor?' the detective said with a glance at the man with the pipe.

'Precisely, to coin a phrase,' Sir Trevor Kirkland said, as he tamped down the tobacco in the worn bowl of his briar with a stubby finger. He gave a good-humoured smile to Dr. Morelle. 'And that's what brought me over on this afternoon's plane.'

'Of course,' Levaque said slowly, 'since Laking had consulted you, who else

would know more about the secrets of his heart than you?'

'Only Dr. Morelle,' Kirkland said. 'But then, few secrets of the human heart, or mind, seem hidden from him.'

'You are being very complimentary,' Dr. Morelle said, and it seemed very clear to Levaque and Kirkland that he accepted the latter's observation as being no more than his due. 'For my part, I am most grateful to you for making the journey.'

'I would like to offer my thanks to you also,' the French detective said. He went on: 'And you feel assured now, Sir Trevor, that the dead man was acting a part for your benefit? That he was no more mentally deranged than you or I, or Dr. Morelle?'

Kirkland drew at his pipe, exhaled a cloud of smoke slowly and said: 'I'm pretty certain of it, now. That is since I've talked with Dr. Morelle and in the light of what's happened.' Levaque gave him a nod, and then the other said good-humouredly: 'As to the poor devil being no more unbalanced mentally than you or I, or Dr. Morelle, I'm sure Dr. Morelle

would tell you that there ain't no such animal as a normal person.'

'If ever I should find such an individual,' Dr. Morelle said, his saturnine features creasing momentarily with a thin smile, 'you can rely upon me to cure him.' And he joined in a little in the laughter of the other two.

So it was that about an hour later, when his wrist-watch indicated that it was approaching half-past eleven, Dr. Morelle reached the ornamental gates of the Villa Midnight and went in, moving with his long raking stride through the scented garden. Like some nightmare-sized bird of prey he paused on the portico steps. He thought he detected a noise near at hand, the scuff of a shoe, the creak of a window opening. Then he decided it was the breeze rasping through the palm-fronds, or perhaps Miss Frayle moving about inside the villa. He had noticed the light in the library and reflected with satisfaction that she was still at work. A fortunate encounter it had been, after all, in the aquarium that morning. He was

smirking a little to himself as he went into the hall.

He was a trifle puzzled by the stillness that greeted him. Surely Miss Frayle must have heard him close the front-door? He could not believe that she was so absorbed in her work as all that.

He had not anticipated being so late, but the time with Kirkland and Levaque at the Hotel Hugo had passed quickly. Dr. Morelle still felt the warmth of pleasure he had experienced when Sir Trevor had informed him over the long-distance telephone from the hospital where he had contacted the other that he would leave by that afternoon's flight to Nice. Dr. Morelle had met him at the airport in his yellow Duesenberg and as he drove him to Monte Carlo, he had learned in detail Kirkland's opinion of the late Ian Laking.

From all that the stocky specialist, who looked so much more like a successful horticulturist than what he really was, had said, Dr. Morelle had begun to feel convinced that the entire proceedings had been a calculated and complex plot on

271

Laking's part, he had apparently taken no one else into his confidence, to attempt to persuade Dyke Fenton to agree to shoot him. All part of a diabolical trick to implicate the latter in an attempted murder, and thus get him out of the way. Laking, it was evident, had been insensately jealous of Fenton, and suspected him of being his wife's lover.

As Kirkland talked to him of the consultation which had taken place, it became crystal clear to Dr. Morelle that Laking had no intention whatsoever of allowing himself to be shot. Not by Fenton or anyone else. His appointment with Kirkland, his strange behaviour, had all been part of a build-up, a plan to have Fenton caught red-handed in the act of attempted murder.

As he turned the idea over in his mind, Dr. Morelle had noted only one weakness in it, which lay in the unknown factor: could Dyke Fenton be persuaded to carry out the arrangement? But that test had never come. Someone had forestalled the plan by murdering Laking before the time when he was supposed to be shot by

pre-arrangement with and by Dyke Fenton. And there was the time element, it was obvious that Laking was counting on his scheme reaching its climax, not tonight, as he had outlined the *modus operandi* to the unsuspecting Fenton, but some time tomorrow.

That could be the only explanation for the deadly, vicious letter he had written which, except for chance, would not have reached Dr. Morelle until tomorrow's post. Or had Laking foreseen in some fashion, which was difficult to comprehend, that the postman would deliver the letter when he did, several hours earlier?

On consideration Dr. Morelle was forced to the conclusion that it couldn't have been the case. It was a matter of pure chance. One of the imponderables which were not so rare in murder-cases where more often than not, some loose ends never were satisfactorily tied up, even when the case was solved.

Another example of the way chance had loaded the dice in the game was that of all persons Laking had been advised by

Kirkland to go to for treatment, it had to be Dr. Morelle.

These and other conclusions and speculations circled Dr. Morelle's mind as he crossed the hall. And then he remembered he had mentioned to Miss Frayle that he expected to be back before dinner. He called out to Miss Frayle as he approached the library, and then he heard the sound. It was a faint moan and as he stood at the door, what he saw brought a grim expression to his face.

His precious papers were scattered all over the exquisite Italian writing-desk, and Miss Frayle was a slumped figure in the chair. As he looked at her she gave a groan and he moved to her quickly. As he saw the ugly bruise above her temple, she gave another groan, her eyes opened and she stared at him blankly, as if she hadn't the faintest idea who he was or what he was doing there. She threw a wildly vague glance about her, and it was plain she didn't know what she was doing there either. Then her eyes behind the horn-rims focussed on him once more, and

became filled with the light of recognition.

'Dr. Morelle,' she said. 'Fancy you being here.'

His voice took on an unusually gentle tone. 'You have no need to feel any alarm, Miss Frayle. It would appear that you have met with a slight accident.'

He saw that the impact of the blow she had suffered had caused an abrasion of the skin, and the discoloration made the wound appear more serious than it really was. Without asking any questions he obtained a glass of iced water which he gave her, and which she drank down gratefully. Next he set about attending to her damaged head.

A few minutes later she was sitting up with a neat dressing over her temple, and the ache over her eye subsiding. 'And now perhaps you feel able to tell me what has transpired.'

She took a gulp at the glass of water and coughed and choked as it went down the wrong way. It had been terrifying. It had happened so suddenly after the light went out that it was hard to remember

exactly what had taken place. Except that she had been attacked. The sight of Dr. Morelle, as he stood there eyeing her with a certain amount of concern was tremendously reassuring however.

'It was wonderful to wake up and find you'd returned, Dr. Morelle,' she said. 'I had been worrying about you, wondering what could have happened to you to make you so late, and then this happened to me.'

He gave a slight cough as he recalled that he had advised her that he would be returning before dinner. He also remembered the noise he had heard when he had arrived, and which he had dismissed as being of no consequence. Had he arrived a few minutes ealier, he might have seen who it was.

She was screwing up her face in a painful effort to concentrate. 'All I got was a glimpse of a hand before the light went out. But I'm sure it was a woman's hand.'

Dr. Morelle frowned at her. He took a Le Sphinx from his slim gold cigarette-case and lit it. 'Tell me everything you can

remember,' he said.

'Mr. and Mrs. Boillot went off, they said you'd promised them they could go to visit their god-child,' he nodded, 'and after tea I went out on the terrace to read a magazine. I dropped off to sleep and when I woke up it was dark.' She gave a nervous laugh. 'It sounds silly, but I was a bit scared. I came in, closed the windows and came in here to work.'

'And how long were you working?'

'I'm afraid I don't really know. You know how absorbed I get.' She smiled at him. 'But after a while I heard a noise. It sounded as if someone was moving about, but I thought it must be you come back.' Her eyes widened as she relived the terror of the next few moments. 'I didn't hear the door open, but something made me look up and I saw a hand switch off the light. I'm sure it was a woman's hand. It was so small and the wrist very slim. She was wearing a black glove.'

'Do continue, my dear Miss Frayle,' Dr. Morelle said through a puff of cigarette-smoke.

She thought he was amused by her

melodramatic description of what had happened. She realized she must have raised her voice as she reached the dramatic bit. She lowered her tone as she went on. 'I was too frightened to move,' she said. 'I called out, but there was no reply. It was very dark and my eyes hadn't got used to it. I couldn't see anything at all. But there was someone in the room with me. It, it was horrible.'

Dr. Morelle gave a nod of objective interest, but there was little sympathy in his expression now, or in his voice as he urged her to proceed with her account.

'I felt her come closer,' she said, with a gulp. 'Then I smelt scent, the scent she was wearing. Expensive scent; I should have thought it was — ' She broke off and then said: 'I was too terrified to move. There was a rustling sound as if she was brushing against the desk. Next I felt a blow on my head and everything went black. I don't remember any more.'

Dr. Morelle had turned away and was staring at the curtained french windows beyond which lay the garden of shadows, quiet now under the stars. Who was it

that had sped that way, a shadow among the shadows, at that moment of his arrival? A woman; Miss Frayle seemed to be positive about that. And yet she had lain unconscious for two or three hours, by the appearance of her injury.

'I just can't understand it,' Miss Frayle was saying to him helplessly. 'What did she want, do you suppose?'

Dr. Morelle reminded her of what he had mentioned earlier in connection with the shooting at the Villa des Fleurs. 'The publisher who was shot in the back?' Miss Frayle said. 'Which reminds me. A Mr. Fenton rang this afternoon. He's one of the people concerned, isn't he? Anyway, he said he wanted to speak to you urgently.'

If Dr. Morelle had heard what she was saying he made no comment, but suddenly he turned back to the desk and pulled out a drawer which was half-open to its full length. The contents had been ransacked as if a minor hurricane had swept over it. 'A letter written to me by the dead man prior to his death, and which I placed here before I went out this

evening, seems to have vanished.'

'I haven't seen it,' Miss Frayle said, staring at him in bewilderment. 'I didn't know it was here.'

'It appears that your assailant did.' Though Dr. Morelle had informed Kirkland of the receipt of Laking's deadly message, he had deliberately omitted to mention it to Levaque. He had decided it would only confuse the detective's speculation, without adding to his prospects of elucidating the case.

Miss Frayle had given a gasp. 'You mean that was the reason for the woman's visit? To get that letter?'

He regarded her sardonically. 'Brilliant, my dear Miss Frayle,' he said. 'I am gratified to learn that your old powers of perception have not deserted you in the interim since you quitted my employ.'

'Oh dear,' Miss Frayle said hopelessly. Her head had begun to ache again. This was just like old times. She might be back at 221b Harley Street. 'But I thought you said the letter accused Mr. Fenton of the murder,' she said.

'That is so.'

'Then why should she want it? This woman, whoever she is?'

But he hadn't appeared to have heard her this time. Miss Frayle blinked as she saw him cross to the door and pause on the threshold. For a heart-stopping moment she imagined he had heard someone out in the hall, her assailant returning, and she opened her mouth to give a squeak of alarm. Then she closed it again as he bent suddenly and picked up something from the floor. She had an impression of a tiny object glinting in the light as it lay in the palm of his hand. Was it something that the intruder had dropped as she'd hurried off, some vital clue?

'If you are so sure it was a woman,' he said to her quietly over his shoulder, 'then the next step is to find her.'

'Yes, Doctor,' she said excitedly. '*Cherchez la femme,* as they say in French.'

28

Stacey Laking had stood on the steps leading from the front door of the Villa des Fleurs to the gardens, where the deep shadows of the trees lay across the path, but now as at last she heard the scrape of approaching footsteps she moved down the steps and called out in a low voice.

Dyke Fenton's voice came from the darkness. Then he was on the steps and she saw his face, deathly white and harassed. She was shocked by the taut expression, the burning, hollow eyes. 'Dyke,' she said, 'you look all in.'

'I've got to talk to you, Stacey. Where's Sara?'

'She's upstairs,' she said, her heart sinking at the hardness of his tone. 'She knows you phoned, but I didn't say you were coming round. She should be asleep. I guessed you wanted to see me alone. Dyke, what happened tonight?'

'I've just left the Villa Midnight,' he said.

He heard her gasp, saw her hands flutter, wraith-like in the starlight. 'You've seen Dr. Morelle?'

'Unfortunately, no.' His smile was grim. 'He wasn't there.'

'I don't understand.' She spoke in a whisper that sounded full of puzzlement. 'You said you were going to phone first,' she said. 'Before you tried to see him.'

He held out his hand to her, she took it in hers. It was icy-cold. They stood at the foot of the steps, the fragrance of the flowers in their nostrils, the rustle of the trees in their ears, and Dyke's voice was low as he told her how he had found himself at the Villa Midnight, almost as if he had been drawn to it unawares. 'I had a surprising reception. Someone whacked me, with one of those blunt instruments.' He touched the painful area that still made his head ache.

'Dyke,' she said. 'Dyke, how awful. Who was it?'

'Search me,' he said slowly. He wasn't looking at her. 'There was a light on, and

I thought Dr. Morelle would be back, so I rang. The hall light wasn't on, so I couldn't see who opened the door to me. I asked for Dr. Morelle. Whoever it was, they just held the door wider. As I went in,' he took a deep breath, 'that was when I bought it. Next thing I knew was a crack on my head. And I went out cold.'

'I can't believe it.' She was staring at him, he could sense her eyes searching his face. His gaze was still turned from her.

'When I came round,' he said, 'the villa was silent. I was alone, at least I thought I was, until I found that secretary of his in the library. She'd been knocked out, too.'

'But why, Dyke, why?' Stacey's eyes were enormous in the moonlight. He was looking at her now. She met his narrowed stare levelly enough.

'I'll give you two guesses,' he said. 'Though you'll only need one. They were after the letter. Remember, Stacey? Ian's letter to Dr. Morelle, fixing me good and proper.'

She said nothing. Fenton could see her run her tongue over her stiff lips. 'I was in a spot,' he said tonelessly. 'If Dr. Morelle

found me he'd think I'd bashed Miss Frayle to get the damned letter back. Whoever had called had turned the writing-desk inside out. And then I heard someone at the front door. It might have been him, it might have been anyone. Levaque himself, for all I knew. And if it was him, I'd have had it and no mistake. I — I had to leave her. I just couldn't risk it.'

'No one saw you leave?'

'No,' he said. Was there an odd note in her question? Or was he beginning to imagine things? 'I ought to phone through to see if it was Dr. Morelle and if the young woman's all right.'

'Who can it have been, Dyke?'

'It was a woman,' he said flatly.

'A woman?' Incredulity widened her eyes, which somehow weren't fixed on him now. 'How do you know?'

'Because,' Fenton said, as he faced Stacey squarely, 'she was wearing scent. I recognized the scent.'

'Ian's letter,' she was saying, 'it wasn't there?' You didn't get it?'

'I didn't get it, no. And so far as I could

tell, it wasn't there. But Dr. Morelle might have had it on him all the time.'

She wasn't listening to him now. Her expression transfixed him. 'You recognized the scent the woman wore?' she said.

'It was yours,' he said brutally. 'I don't know any other woman who uses it.'

Her hands flew to her face. Her eyes closed and she swayed towards him as if she was going to pass out. Involuntarily he made as if to move to her, to take her in his arms. But she turned away and he thought she muttered something about did he think it was she who'd been there.

'I don't know what to think,' he said, utterly sick to his stomach. 'Nothing seems to make sense.' For all the festering suspicion that welled up within him until he felt he would choke, his heart contracted as he heard her broken sob. 'There's only one thing left me,' he said, his own voice sounding as if it was coming from a long way away. 'And that's to get back to Dr. Morelle.'

She gave a cry and her figure taut with the agony of mind that racked her, she

stumbled up the stairs and went into the house. The door slammed behind her. Dyke Fenton made a move after her, then stopped, his fists clenched. Then he swung on his heels and made his way towards the gate. He didn't look back at the villa.

As the door slammed behind her, sounding in her ears like the crash of doom, the woman had paused for a few moments, trying to recover her self-possession. She was looking at the door, and then hearing a movement she turned quickly. Sara stood in the hall. She was wearing the dressing-gown of smart, masculine lines.

'I heard the door,' she said.

'I know. I'm sorry it banged. I couldn't get to sleep. I went out again for a breath of air.'

Sara shrugged. 'You didn't wake me. I haven't been able to sleep, either. I've been wading through the manuscript.' She gave a little smile. 'Sounds like it's one of those you can't put down.' Stacey could feel her gaze on her, intent and searching, and she wondered what she

must be thinking. She felt somehow that the other didn't accept a word of her story about not sleeping and going out again for some air.

Sara found her cigarette case in the deep pocket of her dressing-gown and Stacey took one, wishing she could stop her hand trembling as she held it for Sara to light for her. 'D'you suppose Dyke has seen Dr. Morelle yet?' Sara said.

Was she pretending, Stacey thought, or did she know that Dyke had not long hurried off? In order to give her time to make a non-committal reply, she went into the sitting-room. 'I don't know,' she said. 'I should think so.' She looked at the ormolu clock on the mantelpiece. It was a few minutes past eleven.

'He gave Dyke until tonight to produce the man who did it,' Sara said slowly. 'Then he was going to hand the letter over to that horrid little man.'

Stacey nodded. Would Dyke Fenton carry out his threat, for he had sounded as if it was no less than that, and see Dr. Morelle tonight, tell him everything?

'And didn't he say he was going to the

Villa Midnight,' Sara said. 'When he phoned you?'

Stacey drew on her cigarette without answering. Instead she thought of something to ask the other, she tried to marshal her thoughts to put it into words. She said slowly: 'I've been thinking about the way Ian behaved. The last few months, I mean. Sara,' and she looked at her squarely, 'there wasn't another woman, Sara, was there?'

Sara frowned at her in surprise. 'Why on earth,' she said, 'should you think a thing like that?'

'It's important to know, I mean, if there was another woman, perhaps someone he'd treated badly. Everybody has assumed he was shot by a man.'

Sara interrupted her with a short laugh, then she abruptly checked herself. 'I'm sorry. It's not funny. But you're imagining things. Besides,' she stubbed out her cigarette, 'there's the letter. How could some woman know about that, and act accordingly?'

'She could have overheard Dyke and Ian,' Stacey said. 'The same way we

assumed some man had done.'

'But she still wouldn't have known about the letter,' Sara said insistently.

'There again,' Stacey said, forcing herself to go on talking, her mind was not here, but with Dyke Fenton; was he talking now to Dr. Morelle, or was it Levaque whom he had heard arrive at the Villa Midnight? 'we've taken it for granted Ian wrote it. But — but it's just occurred to me that it could have been a forgery. Someone else could have written it and sent it to Dr. Morelle with the idea of implicating Dyke.'

'A forgery?' Sara said, obviously unimpressed. Stacey thought she pretended to consider it. Then she shook her head. 'That's out of the question. It was in Ian's own handwriting, all right. I know his scrawl, as well as you do.'

Stacey nodded, in her mind's eye now she could see the letter. Dr. Morelle had read it out, being careful not to show it either to her or Dyke, but she had seen the writing through the somewhat transparent paper. It had looked like Ian's.

And then, suddenly, she was listening

to the deathly silence that had fallen between her and Sara, a hush that was charged with an unbearable tension. Sara's face had gone blank, she seemed to be avoiding Stacey's eyes.

With an overwhelming shock Stacey Laking realized what Sara had said. *How could Sara be so positive the letter was in Ian's own handwriting? Only if she had seen it, before he had sent it, or after Dr. Morelle had received it.*

29

Stacey found herself staring at the Colt automatic. 'Said too much, didn't I?' Sara was saying to her pleasantly, only her voice sounded like the waves of the sea in Stacey's ears, distant waves breaking on a far-away shore. 'Opened my mouth too wide.'

Stacey could not find anything to say. She was mesmerized by the flat, sinister glintingly black gun in Sara's hand. Sara's face had hardened, the smile had gone. Her face was a pinched tight mask which seemed to have gone a curious bluish colour by some trick of the light. 'I know Dyke was here tonight,' she said. 'Although you didn't think it worth the trouble to mention it to me. I heard him tell you about what happened at the Villa Midnight. I was listening in the hall with the door open. You were too busy talking to notice. Not that I needed to hear what I knew already. I was there at the time.'

Slowly Stacey was pulling herself together. 'And it was you who overheard him and Dyke yesterday?'

'Of course. That's what gave me the idea. And then I saw Dyke hide this thing away in the chest in the hall.' The gun was steady in her hand, unwaveringly aimed at Stacey's heart.

'Then you shot Ian?' Stacey said incredulously. But with the horrified disbelief that invaded her mind came a stabbing thought that there was something she must do. There was only one thing she could do. Play for time. Keep Sara talking until someone, Dyke, came. If only Dyke would come back, if only he hadn't believed that it was she who'd murdered Ian, shot her own husband.

'I'm surprised Dyke never guessed I'd got it,' Sara was saying calmly. Though she seemed to be controlling herself with an effort. There was a curious rasp in her words as if she found it difficult to breathe. 'I saw it from upstairs. I'd dashed up there just before he came out of the library. I pretended I'd come from my bedroom.'

'But I don't see — ?'

'You don't see why I did it?' There was contemptuous pity in her voice. 'You don't know what he did to my father. You were never interested in how your husband made his money, that he lied and stole.'

It was true, Stacey thought. She had never known how Ian ran his publishing-firm. It had been his dream, his reality. Something she had never shared with him. She had appreciated all the things the money he'd made had made possible; but what was this about Sara's father?

'He swindled my father,' Sara said. Her voice was bitter. 'Ian's own great best-seller, he never wrote it, my father did. He was Ian's cousin. All the sweat and work he put into it, and then Ian got his hands on it. Father was ill, he needed money. He got it, a paltry sum, and then he died.'

'But how do you know all this?' Stacey said in a whisper.

'The original manuscript, I found it after his death. I realized the truth, I sent Ian Laking one page of that manuscript.'

Her eyes glittered at the remembered triumph. 'Since then I've held him in the palm of my hand.'

Dyke would never come, Stacey told herself. Perhaps he was going to telephone instead, she thought wretchedly. But that would be no good.

'He gave me this job, to keep me quiet, plus a cut of the profits,' the other was saying, though Stacey was hardly listening, only prayed she would go on talking.

Sara's eyes were starting with excitement, her lips were bloodless and all around her mouth a bluish colour. There was something she was babbling about how she would benefit by Ian's death. Only Stacey couldn't follow what she was saying. She grinned at Stacey. 'When I heard him and Dyke, then I knew I could settle my father's debt once for all, and I could get to be the boss.'

Stacey could see she was in a curious state of suppressed excitement, her breath was coming in quick gasps, the hand that held the gun trembled a little as if with ague. 'That's why I had to get the letter,' Sara was saying. 'I hadn't known about

that, and I daren't risk Dyke being implicated. I needed him for the firm — my publishing firm. Besides, he was in love with you. I'd guessed that, even though he hadn't. And so you were expendable, Stacey, very expendable. You still are.'

Stacey said, feeling horribly sick: 'And it was you who attacked him tonight?'

'I hope you didn't mind me borrowing your scent?' She giggled, but it was a macabre sound. 'As for that halfwitted secretary of Dr. Morelle's,' she shrugged. 'I knew she was going to be awkward. It was the simplest thing to do.'

Stacey said, her throat dry: 'And now?'

'Now I'm tired, very tired. I want to get this over with.' She made a move forward. 'Turn your back to me.' Stacey stared at her, every muscle in her body rigid, every nerve raw and screaming silently in her brain. She saw that the other was gasping for breath, her face that livid colour. Stacey stood still, facing her squarely.

'I said turn your back to me,' Sara's voice was shrill. 'Curse you, you damned bitch, I don't want you watching me.' She

was shrieking now like someone possessed. Then she made a curious noise in her throat and swayed a little. 'Keep where you are.' The gun had wavered, but with an obvious effort it still kept pointing at Stacey. With her other hand she was searching her dressing-gown pockets, but what she was looking for was not there. Her breath was coming in irregular gasps, her face was blue and pinched. The gun wavered again.

Suddenly there was a movement behind Stacey to her right, the french window opened and Dr. Morelle stepped into the room. He was wearing a dark suit which made him look towering against the terrace and back-drop of stars. His face was bent saturninely upon the scene that met his narrowed gaze. Stacey cried out, Sara twisted. There was a loud report as the gun went off.

As Dr. Morelle started towards her, Sara reeled on her feet, staring at him. He produced something from his pocket which glistened as he held it between finger and thumb for Sara. 'Is this what you require?'

Sara suddenly gave at the knees and fell flat on her face. He crossed to her swiftly, turned the inert figure over. He felt urgently for her pulse, as a last chance broke the glistening ampoule of amyl nitrate which he held and applied it under her nose. There was no reaction. Dr. Morelle folded his handkerchief about the ampoule and then he stood up. 'I was too late,' he said.

'I don't understand,' Stacey said, bewildered. 'Where's Dyke?'

'He is looking after Miss Frayle for the moment. I came here immediately after he'd told me what he knew.' He gave her a thin smile. 'Or what he believed.' She thought his face looked as if it might have been chiselled out of ivory as he glanced at the ampoule and then at the still shape on the floor. 'Amyl nitrate,' Dr. Morelle said quietly. 'She suffered from angina pectoris. I made a mental note of it the first time I saw her. That odd bluish tinge sometimes, particularly in moments of stress, round the mouth. And then I found this, which she had dropped in her hurried exit tonight. The pieces of the

jigsaw fell into place. But you've heard it all from her. It made quite charming listening, I thought.'

'She would have killed me, if you hadn't come.'

'I had to time my entrance like an actor,' he said. 'I had to be sure that gun wasn't aimed at you.' He glanced again at the gleaming object in the handkerchief. 'She always carried one of these with her,' he said very quietly. 'This time she forgot.'

Stacey Laking covered her face with her hands. A clock chimed somewhere in the villa. Twelve strokes echoed on the heavy silence, and then Stacey sensed a movement from the gaunt figure who had appeared so dramatically out of the darkness. She took her hands from her face and started to tell him how thankful she was for the sight of him, and then she saw the spreading blood over his shirt front, like a deadly rose that was blooming terribly fast.

'Dr. Morelle,' she said. 'You've been hit — that shot — '

He tried to reach the curtain drawn

back from the french window, to hang on to it for support. But he failed to make it, and she gave a cry and went to him.

As Dr. Morelle collapsed to the floor another clock somewhere in the villa chimed midnight.

THE END

We do hope that you have enjoyed reading this large print book.

Did you know that all of our titles are available for purchase?

We publish a wide range of high quality large print books including:
Romances, Mysteries, Classics
General Fiction
Non Fiction and Westerns

Special interest titles available in large print are:
The Little Oxford Dictionary
Music Book, Song Book
Hymn Book, Service Book

Also available from us courtesy of Oxford University Press:
Young Readers' Dictionary
(large print edition)
Young Readers' Thesaurus
(large print edition)

For further information or a free brochure, please contact us at:
Ulverscroft Large Print Books Ltd.,
The Green, Bradgate Road, Anstey,
Leicester, LE7 7FU, England.
Tel: (00 44) **0116 236 4325**
Fax: (00 44) **0116 234 0205**

Other titles in the
Linford Mystery Library:

MR. WALKER WANTS TO KNOW

Ernest Dudley

Mr. Walker, the Cockney rag and bone man, is always bumping into other people's troubles. After the murder of old Cartwright in the jeweller's shop, he becomes involved in adventures with his friend Inspector Wedge of Scotland Yard, with the arrest of a crooked police officer, and the escape of Cartwright's killer. Then there is another death — in Mr. Walker's own sitting room — but his problems are just beginning, as he discovers that he himself is a candidate for murder!

SCORPION: SECOND GENERATION

Michael R. Linaker

The colony of deadly scorpions at Long Point Nuclear Plant was eradicated. Or so people thought . . . Over a year later, entomologist Miles Ranleigh receives a worrying telephone call. A man has been fatally poisoned by toxic venom, identical to the Long Point scorpions' — but far more powerful. Miles and his companion Jill Ansty must race to destroy the fresh infestation. But this is a new strain of scorpion. Mutated and irradiated, they're larger, more savage — and infected with a deadly virus fatal to humans. And they're breeding . . .

THE RITTER DOUBLE-CROSS

Frederick Nolan

In Nazi Germany, in 1941, there was a factory in the north German town of Seelze. Though officially its function was a top military secret, it was known to be associated with the manufacture of poison gases. Until a raid put the factory out of action ... Based on fact, this is the story of five men who were parachuted in to Seelze to destroy the chemical plant. But the Gestapo were waiting — and one of the five was a traitor ...

THE TRAVELS OF SHERLOCK HOLMES

John Hall

Secrecy surrounds the supposed death of Sherlock Holmes in 1891 — and his re-emergence three years later. What happened to him during the missing years of his life? This story of those missing years reveals how Holmes foiled his old adversary and became involved in a terrible game; its prize, the mastery of an entire continent — India. Holmes' adventures take him to Tibet, Persia and the Sudan, but as sole representative of the British Government, his life and the British Empire is at stake.

THE PLACE OF THE CHINS

David Bingley

In 1944, Scoop Britwell, British war correspondent, is to be dropped into Burma along with a deployment of commandos, back-up for the fighting, forgotten army. However, a premature crash landing plunges him into the jungle war with the Japanese. Events push him into an heroic role, endearing him to his commando comrades and the loyal Burmese. And when harsh conditions hold back his despatches, there are many willing helpers to his cause at the Place of the Chins.

SPECIAL MESSAGE TO READERS

This book is published under the auspices of

THE ULVERSCROFT FOUNDATION

(registered charity No. 264873 UK)

Established in 1972 to provide funds for research, diagnosis and treatment of eye diseases. Examples of contributions made are: —

A Children's Assessment Unit at Moorfield's Hospital, London.

•

Twin operating theatres at the Western Ophthalmic Hospital, London.

•

A Chair of Ophthalmology at the Royal Australian College of Ophthalmologists.

•

The Ulverscroft Children's Eye Unit at the Great Ormond Street Hospital For Sick Children, London.

You can help further the work of the Foundation by making a donation or leaving a legacy. Every contribution, no matter how small, is received with gratitude. Please write for details to:

THE ULVERSCROFT FOUNDATION,
The Green, Bradgate Road, Anstey,
Leicester LE7 7FU, England.
Telephone: (0116) 236 4325

In Australia write to:
THE ULVERSCROFT FOUNDATION,
c/o The Royal Australian and New Zealand
College of Ophthalmologists,
94-98 Chalmers Street, Surry Hills,
N.S.W. 2010, Australia

D0556685